MODERN

Glamour. Power. Passion.

MILLS & BOON

First Published 2025
First Australian Paperback Edition 2025
ISBN 978 1 038 94042 1

GREEK'S ONE-NIGHT BABIES © 2025 by Lynne Graham
Philippine Copyright 2025
Australian Copyright 2025
New Zealand Copyright 2025

This is a work of fiction. Names, characters, places, and incidents are either the
product of the author's imagination or are used fictitiously, and any resemblance to
actual persons, living or dead, business establishments, events, or locales is entirely
coincidental.

MIX
Paper | Supporting
responsible forestry
FSC® C001695
www.fsc.org

Published by
Harlequin Mills & Boon
An imprint of Harlequin Enterprises (Australia) Pty Limited
(ABN 47 001 180 918), a subsidiary of HarperCollins
Publishers Australia Pty Limited
(ABN 36 009 913 517)
Level 19, 201 Elizabeth Street
SYDNEY NSW 2000 AUSTRALIA

Cover art used by arrangement with Harlequin Books S.A.. All rights reserved.

Printed and bound in Australia by McPherson's Printing Group

Greek's One-Night Babies

Lynne Graham

MILLS & BOON

Lynne Graham was born in Northern Ireland and has been a keen romance reader since her teens. She is very happily married to an understanding husband who has learned to cook since she started to write! Her five children keep her on her toes. She has a very large dog who knocks everything over, a very small terrier who barks a lot and two cats. When time allows, Lynne is a keen gardener.

CHAPTER ONE

THE GREEK TECH tycoon Nic Diamandis was deep in thought as he steered the SUV through what was increasingly looking like a blizzard. En route to his Yorkshire hideaway, he was only vaguely grateful that he was close to his destination. He was preoccupied with the infinitely more distressing family revelations that had been contained in the personal letter the executor had given him after his father's death.

Revelations that had plunged him into a devil's quandary.

In short, his father, Argus, had had an affair with his mother's closest friend, Rhea, and the young woman who was Nic's closest friend was actually his half-sister.

Six months ago, that truth might not have tasted quite so toxic. Indeed, Nic could have happily embraced it because he had always been fond of Angeliki Bouras, his childhood playmate, his adolescent wing woman. But then something had changed…for *her*, at least, if not for him. A month ago, Angeliki had got into his bed when he was half asleep and had made a pass at him. Awakening, he had rejected her in shock at her approach. And... Well, it had pretty much wrecked their friendship because he had not seen her since, and she wouldn't take his calls.

Telling Angeliki now that he was her brother would obviously only increase the fallout from that damaging incident. As for his mother? How could he possibly tell her such news when she was still so close and reliant on Angeliki's mother for emotional support? Hadn't Bianca Diamandis already suffered enough throughout her marriage to a monster? Nic's father, Argus, deserved no other label. He had repeatedly cheated on Nic's mother and humiliated her. He had also lied and conned his way through the business world, destroying those he disliked, bribing others, blackmailing the vulnerable. Argus had never been a father a son could respect and aspire to copy. He had been an abusive bully, securing his status through fear and intimidation. And Nic had always loathed him.

In fact, the only person likely to receive the news that Angeliki was a secret Diamandis without regret or prejudice was Nic's half-brother, Jace. Why? Argus had rejected Jace when his first marriage crashed and burned and Jace had been raised by his uncle instead. Jace had been the lucky *son who got away* and Nic could only envy his older brother for his escape from his own hellish childhood. That past was something he preferred not to think about, but his father's recent death had brought all that emotional stuff he abhorred to the surface again, unsettling him.

Nic slowed his speed as the falling snow grew ever more impenetrable and then sudden movement to the left seized his attention and he watched a tiny vehicle surge across his path and plunge into the field on the other side of the road. He blinked for a split second, fully aware now that he had just seen an accident, and was about to use his phone before common sense forced him to slow his pace and draw the SUV to a careful halt and climb out. After all, he was here on the spot and could possibly even save a life long before any emergency rescue could be enacted. He climbed out, a black-haired, six-foot-four-inch-tall wall of a man, warmly clad for the weather in sturdy boots and an overcoat. He walked back a few yards before spotting the car down the hill, lying on its side in the snow.

Clambering down the steep embankment, he cut across the straggling hedge and made it to the vehicle. It was resting on the driver's side. He opened the hatch at the back, very relieved that it wasn't locked. He yanked out the pink suitcase in his way and heard a woman's gasping sob.

'You're going to be all right. I'm planning to get you free. Are you hurt?' he asked, for it might not be safe for him to try and move her.

He heard her suck in air as though she was trying to get a grip on herself. 'Just bruised and shocked…

I think. The car wouldn't stop. It just kept on going on down the hill and then it speeded up—'

'Doesn't matter. Do you want me to try and get you out? Or do you want me to call the emergency services and wait for them?' Nic asked.

'Oh, no, please just get me out, if you can,' she begged.

'Can you release your seat belt?'

'No, it's too far above me. I can't reach it,' she framed shakily.

'Stay calm. We'll get you out.' Nic swore, shedding his heavy coat as he tried to lever himself into what was surely the smallest car in existence. It was basically a city runabout and totally unsuited to the challenge of snowy and steep country roads.

'Without any jokes about women drivers,' she warned him.

And quite unexpectedly, Nic laughed, appreciating her snarky humour at such a moment. After all, he could tell that she was frightened by her shaky voice but she wasn't giving into the fear, she was fighting it.

'My name is Nic,' he told her. 'What's yours?'

'Lexy,' she mumbled as he stretched up to depress the seat-belt button and it released and she slumped fully against the door below her.

For the first time he saw the driver and no longer wondered why he had had no view of her even from the rear of the car, because she was absolutely tiny, almost child-sized and, on a positive note, she ought to be light enough for him to lift and extract. 'Grab my hand,' he urged, reaching down as close as he could get to her.

'Can I grab my handbag?'

'No.'

'But I can't do anything without my handbag!' she wailed in dismay.

'Right now, we're concentrating on getting *you* out.'

Lexy grabbed the big masculine hand and gasped as he literally hauled her up.

'Grip my shoulder,' he told her, and she complied as he raised her up and she had a blurred vision of bronzed skin, black hair and very dark eyes.

With the muted venting of what sounded like a foreign curse word, he began to manoeuvre the two of them backwards out of the car.

'I can manage now.'

'You told me you weren't hurt and you are,' her rescuer complained, still carefully tugging her onward, his stubborn stubbled jawline prominent. 'There's blood on your face!'

'I think I scraped something when the car went airborne or when the airbags exploded,' she framed unevenly as she was lifted out and set on her feet. Her stiletto heels sank deep into the snow and she shivered, suddenly acutely aware of the thin shirt and smart tailored skirt she wore, garments quite useless in such weather. 'I was trying to get to the airport.' She checked her watch and winced. 'Too late now,' she said.

'At least you're alive and relatively unscathed,' Nic remarked as he grabbed his coat up and draped it round her shoulders to keep her warm. 'Do you really need that bag?'

She was like a miniature oil painting, Nic was thinking, even with the streak of blood from the small scrape on her cheek. She had tousled silky golden hair spilling round her shoulders, delicate little features and a mouth as naturally pink and luscious as a peach. Wide bluey green eyes. Beautiful, just a bit too much on the small side in every direction, he reasoned. Totally *not* his type. He had never gone for blondes. His mother was blonde. Angeliki was blonde. He reminded himself that neither was a natural blonde while wondering why he had to go to such lengths to avoid admitting that a woman attracted him even if she was standing bedraggled and in shock in heavy snow. Was it because she was an accident victim?

Lexy grimaced and groaned. 'No. I can't ask you to go back in there.'

But Nic wasn't listening. He was already halfway back in and he was so tall that with only a little manoeuvring he was able to vault back out again holding the large purple workbag that held her phone, her wallet, her tablet and a hundred other items she didn't think she could live without, even temporarily.

'Thank you so much,' she told him sincerely. 'I have to ring the hire company and tell them I've had an accident.'

'Where are you planning to go now, since the airport is out of reach? It's too far on roads this bad.'

In the back of her mind, the vague hope that *he* might have been able to drop her at the airport died. 'I've got nowhere to go,' she said, in consternation at that fact. 'And I don't know the area. I was at a business conference at a country-house hotel, but that's miles and miles behind me now.'

'There's no accommodation within easy reach around here. It's rather remote.' Nic reached for her case with a frown because he knew he had no choice but to take her back to his place, for the night at least. 'You can stay with me tonight and we'll see about moving you elsewhere tomorrow.'

'With you…er, I don't know you.'

'Or ring the police or a friend, see if they're able to help you,' Nic continued with innate practicality and the simple desire to be gone. 'I'm afraid I can't hang around in this weather in case I can't make it to my place either.'

'I can understand that,' Lexy conceded, in a real tizz of indecision.

The guy had stopped in a blizzard at the scene of an accident and had taken the risk of getting her out of the car she was trapped in. Ostensibly, he was a decent man. Couldn't she take a risk on him? My goodness, was she turning into her excessively anxious and suspicious mother? Seeing threat behind the most innocent façades? For the first time she looked up at him. He was so tall, so broad and…so incredibly good-looking that all of a sudden she couldn't believe he could be a perv. Nobody that handsome needed to be, she thought foolishly, before getting embarrassed by that utterly stupid thought.

She dug shakily into her bag to extract her phone. 'I'll stay with you but, if you don't mind, I'll take a photo of you and your car registration and send it to my friend.'

Nic rolled his eyes and grinned. 'Whatever.'

She snapped a photo as he grabbed her case in one hand and began to stride back over the rough ground. Lexy followed at as close to a run as she could manage in her high heels, her feet already frozen blocks of ice. He paused on the other side of the hedge and stepped back to bodily lift her over it. Her shoes had no purchase on the slippery embankment, and he had to haul her up that as well, his coat trailing on the ground. Her cheeks were burning with mortification at her own lack of physical stamina as he urged her down the road and she saw a large black SUV parked.

'Registration photo,' he reminded her gently when the only thing on her mind was getting into his car and out of the cold.

Lexy laughed at that soothing encouragement for her to document him for her own safety. 'Right.'

Chilled hands clumsy, she snapped the registration plate and, climbing into the passenger seat, she began to remove his coat until he told her to keep it on for warmth. She texted her friend and flatmate, Mel, with brief facts and attached the photos before heaving a sigh because suddenly she felt ridiculously sleepy.

'I'm so tired,' she framed.

'You're coming off an adrenalin high after the accident.

'My house is up here,' Nic intoned only a few miles further down the road, turning the car into a lane surrounded by what appeared to be a small forest. 'I like my privacy. I planted the trees before the foundations were dug.'

'You built your own house?' she asked in some surprise, because he had a smooth, polished edge that made it difficult for her to picture him doing anything that hands-on physical.

His facial muscles tensed. He hadn't meant he had actually planted the trees himself, but he didn't contradict her because an overnight unexpected guest did not require his life story.

Lexy's mouth ran dry in surprise as the driveway opened up to reveal a sizeable modern house that seemed to be mostly glass and wood. It was very elegant and clearly architect-designed. Her host, it seemed, lived at a much higher level than she did. Just as quickly her requiring shelter for the night seemed an even worse imposition.

'I'm really sorry that I'm putting you out like this,' she said awkwardly as she slid out of the car, head bowing in the wind blowing heavy snow at her.

'It's not a problem,' he assured her wryly. 'It's a spacious property.'

On the doorstep she turned aside as he disarmed some security alarm before he ushered her indoors to glorious heat. 'Take the shoes off. Your feet must be wet,' he urged her.

'And they hurt. Definitely not shoes made for walking in,' she quipped, bending down to remove the shoes and set them neatly by the wall before straightening again to take in her surroundings.

Wow, she thought at first glimpse of the metal sculpted starburst lights hanging far above, the sort of signature piece that only a designer created. Double wow, she thought as she noted a sleek bronze sculpture and the stone and metal staircase leading off the big limestone-tiled entrance hall. Triple wow, she thought, feeling the warmth of underfloor heating unfreeze the soles of her feet.

Thee mou, she literally shrank when she took off the heels. Nic stared down at her and realised that she reminded him of a fairy ornament on a Christmas tree. Light, airy, insubstantial in some ethereal way. It made her incredibly feminine. Registering that he was staring, relieved that she hadn't noticed his absorption in her, he looked away, wondering just why he found her so fascinating.

'I'll stow your case in the guest room. It's second left down the corridor,' he advised, tugging open a door into a reception room. 'I suggest you go into the drawing room and warm up by the fire. The cloak-room's across the hall.'

Only rich people had drawing rooms, Lexy reflected uneasily as she tactfully took his advice, rather than follow him around like a tracker. Barefoot, she hurried over to the blaze in the log burner and defrosted in front of it before removing his coat and padding back out to the hall to enter the cloakroom and hang it up. Nothing else hung there and she assumed he lived alone. She freshened up at the sink, critically studying her wan, anxious expression in the mirror, dabbing away the streak of blood to note the tiny cut below her cheekbone. She had been lucky, really, really lucky, not to suffer a more serious injury, she reminded herself as she drove a brush through her long snarled-up hair and winced, reckoning that she had a bump at the side of her head.

Tugging out her phone, she made the necessary calls, one to the car-hire firm to report the accident and the location of the car and the second to her boss, Eileen, who ran the interpreter/translator company where she worked, to explain that she was currently marooned in the snow. There was a text from her friend, Julia, reminding her of her pick-up time in thirty-six hours for her lift down to Cornwall with

Julia's mother. She winced, afraid she wouldn't make it back to London in time because of the weather. But she decided not to warn Julia of her current predicament and stress her out. A godmother had to turn up at a christening, after all, when it was such an honour to be chosen. Even so, Lexy was still surprised by her own selection for the role as she had only seen Julia once since university, after her friend had dropped out, married and moved to the country.

Warning her boss had been automatic even though her absence was unlikely to affect business, Lexy reflected wryly, as she received less work than some of her colleagues. The languages she specialised in, Korean and French, were not in as high demand as the likes of Spanish or Chinese would have been. Of course, it wasn't as though she had had much choice about the languages she had acquired through her own background, she conceded wryly.

Lexy had grown up in South Korea, where her banker father worked, and her French-speaking mother had provided her with her second language. Her decision to study languages had been purely practical. After her parents' contentious divorce and her mother's subsequent breakdown following their return to the UK, finding stable employment as soon as possible had been her sole motivation. She had studied for her language degree while working in an unofficial capacity whenever Eileen requested her services at the same time as working numerous jobs in the catering trade to make ends meet.

And at the end of the day, where had sacrificing her own choices got her? That unwelcome thought slunk in no matter how hard she tried to stifle it. Her mother had passed away in any case, unable to appreciate her daughter's efforts to sustain her, exhausted by the agonies of living without domestic staff and without a man to tell her what to do. Admittedly, Agathe Taylor had been a fragile personality. The most daring thing she had ever done had been to marry a much older man against her parents' wishes.

Lexy had never met her late mother's French family but had since learned that they too were dead. Her mother's sense of failure after the divorce had been strong enough to ensure that Agathe had not wished to get back in touch with her relatives. As for her father's family, they were now fully engaged with his much younger second wife and the son he had long craved. A son as opposed to a daughter, Lexy, whom he had never wanted. And he had not even attempted to hide those feelings from his daughter, ensuring that Lexy was always aware of his disappointment in her.

Suppressing those wounding memories, Lexy emerged into the hall to find her host waiting for her.

'I'll show you to your room. Like me, you probably want a shower, after your…experience,' he assumed.

Lexy simply assumed he wanted her out from under his feet in his own home, a reality she could easily understand. Her cheeks warmed with embarrassment as she questioned whether or not to make the offer she had already decided on.

'I was planning to offer to make dinner as a thank you for your help...that is, assuming there's food in the larder,' she admitted uncomfortably.

From his great height, Nic gazed down at her and paused. 'That would be very kind of you,' he told her, unable to suppress that generous response when he saw the anxious light in her clear ocean-coloured eyes. It wasn't the moment to tell her that he was a perfectly capable cook in his own right.

Geographical distance from his domineering father had given him a freedom he could never have enjoyed in Greece. As a business student in London, he had refused the large staffed apartment and the security that Argus had tried to force on him, protesting that he wanted a more normal experience than the Diamandis wealth had allowed him growing up. Argus had scoffed because he had always revelled in showing off his 'richer than King Midas' status and the bragging rights that went with it. Nic, on the other hand, didn't think he could have become half as successful as he had since been without that grounding understanding of how more ordinary people lived.

'I'll get changed first,' Lexy told him cheerfully, a huge smile transforming her formerly tense face. It reminded him of sunshine breaking out after rain and warmed him.

* * *

The big, elegant guest room was as impressive as the foyer and the drawing room. She opened her case and extracted what she needed to explore the private bathroom. Everything was the very last word in luxury. My word, who was this guy? A movie star with the bank account to match? If he was, she didn't recognise him. Certainly, he had the looks to follow such a career.

She had been close to mesmerised when she'd looked up at him in the hall because he was *that* good-looking. The stop-you-in-your-tracks-to-stare variety. Blue-black hair, flopping damply against his brow, showcasing perfect brows and a straight, equally perfect nose, not to mention the high cheekbones of a model and a full, superbly modelled mouth. Maybe he *was* a model, Lexy reasoned. Or just a random gorgeous guy!

For goodness' sake, why was she fangirling over him? Well, she could answer that with ease. He was definitely the most handsome man she had ever met, she conceded as she walked into the marble enclosed shower and sheepishly abandoned her own shampoo and conditioner to make use of the much fancier products on offer there for a guest.

It was not as though her life to date had allowed her to gain much experience with the opposite sex. Studying, working and looking after her depressed and distraught parent had consumed Lexy's life from the age of fifteen when her father had first dropped the bombshell that he'd wanted a divorce and immediately departed, leaving them marooned in London on what her mother had innocently believed was a holiday. And it *was* only a year since her late mother had passed away, leaving Lexy free of concern for the first time in years but also distinctly lonely. After all, she had deeply loved Agathe even while she was guiltily wishing her parent would grow a backbone in her dealings with her husband. Agathe had subscribed to the conviction that a husband was to be waited on hand and foot and never ever challenged. Unsurprisingly, she had received poor treatment in return for her near worship of her other half and that had included being ripped off in the divorce that had followed.

Lexy had become wary of men after growing up on the sidelines of her parents' dysfunctional relationship. Her father had been scary, cold and a strict disciplinarian. He might not have wanted a daughter but, once he'd had one, she'd had to be perfect in every way from her exam results to her appearance. She shuddered at the very thought of how he would have controlled her had she been a more challenging teenager before he'd departed their lives, but luckily he had been gone by the time she'd developed any rebellious tendencies and her mother had been too lost inside her own head to care what her daughter did, never mind what she wore.

But, even then, Lexy had had too many real-world problems to handle to act like a normal teenager. It had been Lexy who'd had to worry about how the rent was paid, food was bought or what school she attended because her mother might have been there in body, but she had never been there in spirit. Lexy hadn't had the time to crush on pop idols when by the age of fifteen she'd been an illegal kitchen worker in the back of a local restaurant, toiling all hours to pay bills her mother had ignored.

Only when Lexy had finally graduated to earn a decent wage had she had the time to date, and there just hadn't been anyone out there, give or take the occasional randy junior chef giving her the eye and making a move. So, it really wasn't any wonder that she was still inexperienced enough to be fangirling over her fanciable host, she decided ruefully.

After drying her hair, she pulled on the yoga pants and tee she had packed for the previous night but not got to wear because the business conference had run into overtime. Feeling fresh and reaching for her bag, which she went nowhere without, she walked back to the hall. It was already dark and through the glass she could see the snow piling up against the windows. She frowned.

'The snowfall is very heavy,' she remarked anxiously when she heard a sound behind her.

'Yes, it's quite a storm. Would you like a drink?' She flipped round to see Nic standing in the doorway of the drawing room. 'You might as well relax as there's nothing we can do about the weather.'

'You're right,' she conceded with a little nod of her head.

'Drink? I have pretty much everything,' he reminded her with a slanting smile that made her heart go bumpety-bumpety-bump straight away.

'White wine would be good,' Lexy responded, feeling the heat rise in her face and hoping he didn't notice.

Fortunately, he turned away and she followed him back into the very fancy big room, still barefoot because she had not thought to pack any other footwear for the hotel and no way was she forcing her feet back into the heels!

The wine came from a built-in chiller cabinet and she tried not to stare, but she felt as though she were visiting royalty because who else might have a disguised chiller in their drawing room? She accepted her wine glass with a tense smile and sank down on the edge of a plush armchair, knowing that if she sat back properly her feet would dangle like a kid's.

'So you were up here on a business trip,' he remarked casually.

'Yes. I was attending a conference as an interpreter for a South Korean tech firm,' she imparted with greater calm. 'I speak Korean and French. I spent the first fifteen years of my life in South Korea because my father worked in Seoul.'

'Interesting,' Nic commented, studying her with an intensity that made her feel slightly uncomfortable. *Thee mou*, she was gorgeous, he was thinking, scanning her pale perfect skin, her sparkling ocean-coloured eyes and her golden hair. There was something about her face that he found hard to look away from and she was reddening again like a traffic light. He focused on the drink in his hand instead, marvelling at his inept behaviour in such circumstances.

'Maybe you could show me out to the kitchen,' Lexy almost whispered.

'I apologise for staring,' Nic countered easily. 'You're impossibly pretty but I assure you that I am not about to do anything about it that could make you feel unsafe.'

Lexy laughed and said, without even thinking about it, 'I wish I could promise the same!'

Nic gazed back at her with stunned dark-as-night eyes, framed by lush velvet black lashes, narrowing.

Lexy turned hot pink and exclaimed, 'Because you're impossibly pretty too and I wouldn't want *you* to feel unsafe!'

'Kitchen,' Nic reminded her, thinking it was time to end this particular conversation.

CHAPTER TWO

NIC HAD EXPERIENCED every possible type of encouragement from women since he was around fourteen. But...

'Nobody has ever called me pretty before,' he heard himself say, regardless of his previous desire to conclude that dialogue. Lexy was now busily slamming through kitchen cupboards, checking the extensively stocked pantry and investigating the contents of the fridge in a sudden surging hive of industry.

'Well, they mustn't have taken a real good look at you, then,' Lexy mumbled, cheeks on fire as she established that Nic had a surprisingly refined spice rack and every possible tool in what was probably her dream kitchen.

Determining that he had no allergies, she pulled out vegetables, washed them and began to chop them up.

'I'm *not* pretty,' Nic informed her with huge conviction.

'Whatever you say.' He so *was*. She was mortified that she had said what she was thinking out loud, but she knew in her bones that she was safe with him because he had gone out of his way to ensure that she felt secure by allowing her to take those photographs with her phone.

She was ashamed that she didn't have any of the flirtatious chatter that women of her age usually had. She felt clumsy and unfeminine in his presence even though he had labelled her impossibly pretty. And that statement alone made her entire body sing a chorus of appreciation because compliments of that magnitude did not come her way. Not when she had grown up with a father who had once derided her because she lacked his height and, even though she had inherited his colouring, had failed to shine at maths or sports. Those criticisms had hurt like so many other of her father's little asides had done over the years, whittling away at her self-esteem, driving a need in her to support her loving mother in any way she could.

Nic stood in wonderment while she chopped at the speed of a professional chef and expertly threw together a beef stir fry flavoured with spices he had never used. Yes, he could cook, but not as it seemed *she* could.

'Did you learn to cook in South Korea?' he asked.

'No, I learned in the UK. You're seeing the results of seven years of part-time off-the-books employment in a restaurant kitchen. I started out washing dishes and peeling veg and by the time I left, I was good enough to function as a junior chef.'

'What age were you when you started?'

'Fifteen… Yeah, I know it was illegal, but my mum and I needed the money.'

'Didn't she work?' Nic was frowning.

Lexy shrugged a thin shoulder. 'She wasn't really able to. She was depressed after her divorce.'

Nic groaned. 'I know the damage a bad marriage does,' he surprised her by admitting. 'I used to urge my mother to divorce my father, but she thought divorce was a fate worse than death, so I can relate to some degree. But your mother was the adult, she shouldn't have left you to take care of the problems.'

'Why not? Mum had never worked a day in her life. She got married at eighteen and went straight into a set-up where a housekeeper did everything for her and my dad told her what to do the rest of the time. She couldn't cope without money… She didn't know how,' Lexy confessed as she drained the rice.

Seated at the kitchen island on a bar stool, Nic looked at the colourful plate of food set before him and accepted the implements she passed him. 'This looks amazing.'

'No need to over-egg the pudding,' she quipped. 'A guy like you living in a house like this…well, I bet you're not used to bad food.'

For the first time in his life, Nic wanted to deny that reality, wanted to be able to sincerely empathise with a woman, and yet he, a Diamandis from birth, couldn't. He had been born into a very wealthy

Greek dynasty of high achievers. He had developed his first app at university and made a fortune out of it. He might have learned to cook as a student, but he had never in his life had to worry about paying for anything. Everything he had ever wanted was his... except a happy family, something he had longed for as a kid, growing up in a very tense and often hostile atmosphere, striving to avoid his perpetually angry and argumentative and violent father and his demands as best he could. But that was something he *could* share and at least it would get them off the controversial money topic.

'My father ruined my childhood by continually demanding that I compete against my half-brother from his first marriage. He was obsessed with me surpassing him and my brother is a clever guy and that wasn't easy,' he confided.

Her delicate brows pleated, blue-green eyes as wide and open as the Greek sky. She struck him as strangely blunt for a woman, unsophisticated, and yet she had a charm all of her own because he knew he was fascinated and he had always believed that it would take a very special woman to fascinate him. Yet here she was, the very first to do so and she appeared to have no womanly wiles whatsoever, which Nic considered even odder. He was accustomed to women who were only frank about sex but quite happy to lie, blur the truth and fake everything else in an effort to impress him. The name Diamandis was like a dramatic price tag wherever he went, signifying the riches his family had acquired over generations of inherited wealth.

'Why would he have wanted his two sons to compete with each other?' she asked in confusion.

'Because he didn't raise my brother and he didn't see him either. In fact, he acted like he hated him, yet it was very important to him that I performed better than my brother did, which was a serious challenge.'

'Parents can be weird,' she acknowledged as she ate and sipped her water, having refused more wine. 'When my father divorced my mother, he tried to rid himself of responsibility for me as well, telling the judge that he shouldn't have to pay support for me because he had never had much of a relationship with me. Of course, that didn't fly, but the money he did have to pay was a drop in the ocean to him. It was as if, once he decided on the divorce, he wanted to put Mum and me *both* behind him as if we'd never existed.'

'How did we end up talking about deep stuff like this?' Nic enquired, elevating one ebony brow like a question mark. 'More wine?'

'No, thanks.' Lexy busied herself filling the dishwasher, wiping up.

'You cooked. I should clean up.'

'But you're still *sitting* there so you're not *that* keen to muck in!' Lexy shot back at him without hesitation.

His amused dark eyes danced like black diamonds

in starlight and he grinned. 'Rumbled,' he conceded, wondering when a woman had last treated him like a regular man and indeed if it had ever happened before. Billionaires didn't get teased or mocked by women very often.

In fact, thinking about it, Nic could not recall a single woman treating him with anything less than deadly gravity when he spoke. He got special treatment. He didn't get called out on his quirks, his oversights, his short temper or his impatience. Everybody handled him with kid gloves as though he were a precious fifteen-carat diamond.

Lexy felt as though she was reeling from that wicked grin of his. It wasn't just his striking good looks, she reasoned hesitantly, it was more something to do with that insanely compelling smile of his. It unleashed girlie butterflies in her tummy, left her strangely breathless and just about destroyed whatever brain power she possessed. Disconcerted by her own reaction, she turned away again and began to clean the counters, finding occupying her hands a great remedy for her increasing self-consciousness.

Her reactions made her feel like a stupid adolescent, too innocent for her own good. But she wasn't innocent, only in the most basic physical way, she thought ruefully. Being a virgin who had never even been on a proper date was humiliating. Sooner or later, she would have to move her life on in that line, but it would have to be with someone who was genuinely interested in her, someone with some even small degree of caring towards her. She had no plans to waste her time or her body on some guy looking only for a one-night stand. *Or had she?* Shooting a side-wise glance at Nic, she reckoned that if it were him, she could probably consider the idea, because she had never been so attracted to anyone before and opportunities didn't exactly come knocking on her door.

'Let's move upstairs. I have a cosier reception room up there with a terrific view.'

Lexy laughed. 'Is this your "come up and see my etchings" speech?' she joked.

'No, those immortal words have never passed my lips.' Nic grabbed the wine and a couple of glasses. 'More in the realms of Netflix and chill.'

'Well, it's not like your terrific view is likely to be visible in the dark,' she pointed out quietly.

'I don't tell lies,' Nic declared as they reached the top of the imposing staircase and she was shocked enough by the room that lay before her to gasp in de-lighted astonishment.

With only the flickering light of the log burner in one corner, the room was basically all glass, all view, and she could see the snow and the stars and the moon. It was absolutely beautiful, like some sur-real dream. 'This is amazing.'

'I built it for the view.'

'Yet you don't live here the whole time, do you?' she said quite naturally.

Nic flashed shrewd dark eyes to her tranquil face. 'Why do you have that idea?'

Lexy shrugged, quite blind, it seemed, to his suspicion. 'It doesn't seem that lived in. It just doesn't have the vibe or any existing clutter. Initially I thought it could be a luxury let but then you had said you planted the trees, so I knew that wasn't right. So I thought maybe you travelled a lot for work.'

'I do,' Nic conceded, relaxing again as he hit a button to reveal the television screen and handed her the remote. 'Pick your own personal poison. I'm feeling generous.'

Nobody could have been more surprised than Nic when she put on an ancient episode of *Friends*. 'I thought for sure you'd put on a reality show… This is really old,' he complained.

'But this is more relatable than gorgeous chicks in bikinis at exotic locations…or baking or fashion. I watched it growing up. It's my comfort choice.'

'I wasn't allowed to watch TV growing up. My father was convinced it would interfere with my studies.'

'Sounds like he was…a bit of a pain?'

'A lot of a pain,' Nic countered, sinking down on the sofa beside her.

Every so often, Lexy's attention strayed from the giant screen to the snow still falling heavily beyond the glass.

'Stop worrying. We're not trapped.'

'Your car is getting buried,' she contradicted.

'I'll leave next week regardless of how deep the snow is,' Nic murmured soothingly.

'Next week isn't tomorrow.'

'But you don't work at the weekend, do you? I assure you that you won't be trapped here for days,' he responded calmly.

'You don't freak out often, do you?'

Nic sent her another brash grin. 'How did you guess?'

His lack of concern soothed her. Her mother had fretted constantly about every little thing after the divorce and to some extent that habit had threatened to infiltrate Lexy as well.

'Is Lexy short for Alexandra or Alexandria?' he asked.

'Neither. It's Alexander on my birth certificate.'

'Assuming that you were born a girl—'

'I was. But my father was wanting and hoping for a boy and he wouldn't change the name he had chosen,' she admitted stiffly.

'This is actually quite funny,' Nic conceded of the programme, choosing not to comment on what he could see was a sore subject.

'I hate to say I told you so,' she teased.

And then Nic convulsed over one of Joey's lines and Lexy bounced on the seat and punched the air. 'Told you so…told you so!' she crowed like a kid.

Nic rested his hands on her slight shoulders as she turned to him. 'Smug, aren't you?'

Her eyes widened as she looked up at him. Even sitting beside him, she was still looking up and just as suddenly she was almost drowning in the velvet darkness of his spectacular eyes. There was nothing else in the world at that particular moment. It was as if time just stopped dead for her, freezing her in place.

Long brown fingers lifted to her cheekbone and spread at a slow cautious pace. 'Is this all right with you?'

A helpless giggle erupted from Lexy. 'Is this what happens when you tell a guy he's impossibly pretty?'

Nic's wicked smile flashed out. 'I think it must be…'

His mouth covered hers and his lips were unexpectedly soft. Not rough, not aggressive. But who was she kidding? It was only her third ever kiss. There would have been more had her mother not had hysterics when Lexy had tried to leave their little rental flat in male company. In the end men had proved to be too much hassle for her when she had already been struggling to cope with her mother. And why was she even thinking about such stuff when Nic was kissing her? Presumably he couldn't tell that it was only her third kiss.

'You taste amazing,' he said thickly against her parted lips.

Yes, amazing just about covered him as well, she

thought helplessly as he pried her lips apart and went off on an exploration that made her shiver and sent a wave of heat she had never experienced before shooting up through her. His lips teased, his tongue stroked her lip line and then delved inside to provide more intense sensations. She was feeling way more than she had ever expected to feel from a single kiss. Her breasts felt heavy, swollen, her nipples prickling points and that wicked growing heat pooled in her pelvis.

'You're good at this…' she framed, struggling to catch her breath.

'I've been on a learning curve since I was fourteen.'

'That's young.'

'It wasn't in my circle,' Nic husked, gathering her slight body close, edging her carefully onto his lap, gripped by a seething desire as ironically new to him as it was to her and faintly spooked by it. In one strike, she hit every one of his sexual buttons, unleashing a craving that inflamed him, and it was infinitely more exciting than any female possibility he had met with in years.

But he was a playboy, like his big brother, Jace, he reminded himself. He did not have the yacht that his late father had dubbed 'the whorehouse on the seas' but he was far from being boyfriend material. And yet the appeal of those ocean eyes when she looked up at him? In a weird way it knocked him sideways. Even so, he was only twenty-seven and he had no plans to settle down for years and years... There, death of that worrying thought train of association.

He slid a hand below her loose tee shirt and discovered that she wore no bra. He cupped the warm, soft weight of her pouting breast and rubbed the pointed nipple greeting him. She gasped out loud and it was the sweetest sound he had ever heard. It turned him on so hard and fast he pushed against the zip of his jeans. He could barely credit the strength of his own response.

Lexy was being engulfed by a tangle of conflicting reactions. Her body was so on board with his every move that it was simply willing him on to the next step. Her brain was dimly echoing her mother's warnings about men, something crazy about why would a man buy a cow when the milk is free, a hangover from her mother's generation and out of step with current mores. But at the end of the day, it was simply sex, she reminded herself even though her emotions felt much more intense than that belief suggested. It was a bodily thing, not a mental thing.

She didn't need to tie herself up in knots about something so basic and naturally she was curious because the touch of his fingers on her breast was magically arousing. And when he used his mouth there as well, it was even better, like a hot wire tightening between her breasts and the juncture of her thighs.

It made her squirm, it made her needy and she was entranced by those responses.

Her tee shirt glided over her head and vanished. He laid her down on the wide, soft sectional sofa and began to gently divest her of her remaining clothes. If it hadn't been so dark, she would have felt more exposed and shyer, but the only light in the room was the flickering flames of the log burner because he had switched off the TV. Outside the snow was falling in the most hypnotic style, big fluffy flakes drifting down beyond the glass, while all was cosy and warm and calm indoors. It felt magical to Lexy, absolutely magical, just as a dream would be with a gorgeous guy, a gorgeous house, and that gorgeous guy miraculously wanted *her*.

'This feels special,' Nic murmured softly, spectacular dark eyes locked to her. '*You* feel special. Do you want me right now? Or would you rather...wait?'

And Lexy stared up at him in wonderment, it being her conviction that no man would ever offer to defer his own pleasure to please a woman. She smiled, wide and bright then, at being proved wrong. 'I want you now,' she told him gently.

'Contraception?' he asked.

'No, I'm not on anything.' Lexy could feel her cheeks burning as he leant down to her. 'And I haven't done this before.'

His perfect ebony brows drew together. 'Haven't done what before?'

'Sex,' she said simply.

Comprehension tautened his lean bronzed features, followed by bewilderment.

'Don't look at me like that!' she said sharply. 'I just never had that freedom until Mum passed.'

Nic lowered himself down to her and kissed her breathless, struggling to slow the pace down to give her the treatment she deserved. 'I was surprised, not critical.'

That kiss connected Lexy again. She stretched up to him as he began to remove her last garments, hunger twisting through her, making her restless. He shimmied down over her body and spread her thighs and she just about had a heart attack when she realised what he planned to do. It was something she had read about in steamy books, not something she had ever fancied on her own behalf, and she went rigid.

'No,' she told him shakily.

'You'll like it,' Nic swore with sensual resolution. 'Please…'

It was the 'please' that seduced her. If he was willing to say that word in return for doing *that*, she couldn't say no. In any case, shouldn't she explore every possibility? This night was one night out of time between two strangers and it would never be repeated. Ten to one, during the night, the snow would vanish and he might drop her off somewhere and she would never see him again…*ever*. The prospect of never ever seeing Nic again left her chest feeling scarily hollow and she suppressed the thought of that scenario as soon as it appeared.

Breathtakingly exquisite sensations seized her. Yes, just as he had forecast, she liked every glide of his tongue, every lingering attention to the most sensually aware nub in her entire body. Her heart thundered in her ears and the cascade of feelings rose in a blinding wave and a climax shuddered through her, shaking her inside out.

'Don't you dare say I told you so,' she warned him breathlessly.

Nic grinned that smile that whipped her into the clouds and back with its charisma. 'I'm not stupid… I simply want to make this as good for you as it will be for me,' he murmured soft and low.

His sensual lips descended on hers again and a big hand curved over the pouting mound of her breast, skilful fingertips stimulating the beaded tip. The first spark of anticipation was rekindled at that moment. Lexy drew in a stark breath and surrendered to sensation.

When he slid between her slender thighs, she was on a high. His sensual attentions had provided her body with a slick welcome and he eased into her with care. Initially that feeling of fullness stretching her untried depths was both unnerving and stimulating and then he settled deeper and there was a sharp, tearing pang of pain that made her gasp in dismay. He stopped, gazed down at her with those incredibly warm dark eyes and leant back from her and shifted position to kiss her again, carrying her through that moment.

She felt his heartbeat. She felt him move inside her and the thrill of anticipation gripped her when she discovered that there was a wild hunger within her demanding more. It was a need, a desire she had never known before, and it was remorseless and overwhelming. His every potent thrust sent sensation shimmying through her taut body and a pool of liquid heat began to burn at her core. Her heart slammed inside her chest. She couldn't catch her breath as the wild tension built into a fierce, driving need. The excitement seething through her climbed to an almost unbearable level and then, with no warning, as it seemed to her, she was suddenly hurtling over the edge into wave after wave of glorious pleasure again. Nic shuddered in the circle of her arms and groaned.

In the silence of the aftermath, she couldn't quite credit what she had done or what she had just experienced. 'That was...' Words failed her.

'Wonderful,' Nic slotted in thickly, releasing her from his weight only to tug her back into his arms and drop a kiss on her brow that made her smile drowsily. 'You're about to fall asleep on me now.'

'Trying not to,' she mumbled. 'But it feels like it has been the longest day of my life...'

'You're sleeping in my bed with me tonight. I'm

telling you now while you're still awake and capable of objecting.'

Lexy tried to lift eyelids that felt as though they had weights attached to them and swallowed back a yawn. 'Don't care where you put me,' she framed. 'As long as it's not out in the snow.'

Nic laughed but she was already going limp in his arms. He studied her tranquil face in helpless fascination because he was feeling things he had never felt before. Selfish though it would be, he was actually tempted to wake her up because he wanted to get to know her better. He wanted her company. When had that ever happened to him with a woman before? Or when had he ever felt so protective that he refused to wake up an exhausted woman? When, furthermore, had he ever cuddled one after sex? The more he thought about his own behaviour, the more bothered he was by it. What had happened to playing it cool? His normal approach? And why had it seemed so important to get her into *his* bed? After all, he always slept alone and never gave any woman the chance to assume that anything more than sex was on offer.

He stood upright, naked, tugged his jeans back on and then lifted her limp body up into his arms. He wanted her to sleep in comfort. Why did he care about that? Frowning, he headed through the connecting door into the master suite and carefully laid her on his giant luxurious bed, where he surveyed her from all angles with frowning curiosity. He didn't even want to leave her alone, which shook him even more. She was definitely making him feel weird.

Lexy woke up during the night and slid out of bed, pulled on Nic's discarded tee shirt and crept quiet as a mouse through the house to pour herself a glass of cold water. One glass of wine and tiredness had wiped her out very early in the evening, she thought in embarrassment. But she had no regrets, none at all. What if it wasn't to be *only* one night that he wanted? The thought slunk in and as quickly she squashed it again, afraid of being naïve. She was cautious in acknowledgement of her inexperience with men.

A sound behind her made her spin nervously. Clad in only his unbuttoned jeans, Nic lounged in the doorway. Her disconcerted gaze collided with liquid black enticement and she could feel her face burning as if it were on fire.

'You are *so* shy,' he breathed in amusement.

'I'm not... I'm not!' Lexy protested, throwing her head high, bringing up her chin as he slowly folded his arms round her and drew her close. The scent of him flared her nostrils. Clean, warm, masculine, already achingly familiar, as if he had somehow imprinted his being on her.

'I don't even know your surname!' she shot at him, discarding the cool front she would have preferred to show him.

'Diamandis.'

'Well, how do you spell that?' she asked huffily into his chest, knowing that it didn't really matter what his name was as long as he was there for her.

He spelt it out with precision. 'You sleep like the dead,' he informed her.

'I'm not going to argue about that,' she agreed with a flare of amusement driving off her previous drowning discomfort with him.

'Are you hungry?'

'No…but I'm not sleepy either. I must've slept for eight hours,' she pointed out.

Nic stared down at her with brooding intensity. 'Women don't usually fall asleep on me.'

'I can only suppose that's because they didn't have to get out of bed at four in the morning the day before yesterday to make a flight to work,' Lexy told him cheerfully. 'And then miss out on essential meals because my language skills were required during those hours as well, work late that night and present myself at seven a.m. for another shift yesterday. No, I'm not about to apologise for sleeping like the dead.'

Nic grinned in delight at that pithy comeback. 'I'm getting that message.'

'And *I'm* getting the message that you're one of those terrifying high-maintenance guys, who expects to be the centre of attention at any hour of the day.'

Faint colour darkened his sculpted cheekbones and his eyes narrowed. *High maintenance?* 'Of course I'm not.'

'Don't believe you,' she told him truthfully.

An involuntary grin slashed Nic's wide sensual mouth. Surprisingly he liked her sass, the insistence that she wasn't overly impressed by him, and not a flicker of recognition had crossed her face after he'd told her his name. 'I can see I'll have to get persuasive,' he teased, bending down to lift her off her feet.

'What on earth?' she exclaimed.

'I'm carrying you back to bed to prove that I'm *not* high maintenance.'

'All that proves is that you're bossy and you like your own way.'

His dark eyes glinted like molten honey and he frowned. 'No points for romance?'

'You're trying to be romantic?' she exclaimed in disbelief.

'For the very first time in my life and… *Thee mou*, you make it a challenge, *chriso mou*.'

'What language is that?' she prompted as he carried her up the stairs and he noticed that she wasn't objecting and that made him smile again.

'Greek. I'm half-Greek, half-Italian,' Nic imparted. 'But Greek comes most naturally to me.'

As he came down on the bed with her still gathered in his arms, she rested her cheek momentarily against his bare chest, revelling in the scent of his skin, the soft brush of the black curls of hair sprinkling his pectoral muscles. 'We have one small problem,' he divulged.

'What is it? Oh, my word, are you married or something?' she demanded in sudden horror, already striving to move off his lap.

Strong arms tightened round her to hold her in place. 'Don't be silly. I've never been married, engaged or committed to any woman.'

'Ever?' she stressed in stricken consternation at that admission.

'Not committed, but...' Nic shrugged a smooth brown shoulder, suddenly at a loss for words because it was way too soon to say anything even though he already knew that, come the dawn, he wouldn't be done with Lexy '...that could change at any time with the right woman.'

'The problem you mentioned,' she reminded him, relaxing a little more again, knowing in her bones, without knowing how, that he was referring to her.

'I only had one contraceptive in my wallet. I don't bring women here. You're the first. So, we will have to practise extreme caution when we get back into bed together again,' he warned her.

'Caution is fine,' Lexy told him sunnily. 'You get het up about the silliest things.'

'If you say so.'

And then he was sliding her into the bed while kissing her breathless and that fast, she wasn't thinking any more. It was the burn of his mouth on hers, the sizzling heat and growing ache at the heart of her and the wondrous caress of his hands that drove everything else out of her head. Although she had sworn she had had sufficient sleep, at some stage of their prolonged intimacy she drifted off again, comfortable and secure in his arms. The one thing she would later remember in detail, and loathe, was that at that moment she felt incredibly safe for the first time in years and quite ridiculously happy.

CHAPTER THREE

NIC SHOOK HER AWAKE, hauled up her pillows, physically lifted her up to rest back on them and murmured, 'Good morning...'

Lexy blinked before the unfamiliar surroundings locked into place and then centred on him: tall, dark, even more good-looking in harsh daylight than he had been in semi-darkness and the warmth of flickering flames. And she smiled, her heartbeat quickening as he slotted a tray onto her lap with the air of a man who had achieved something important to him.

'Breakfast in bed?' she gasped, not having to work at her stunned reaction at that much attention.

'To prove that I'm not only *not* high maintenance but also a reasonable cook,' he shot back at her with amusement glimmering in his honey-gold eyes, which were not quite as dark in bright light. Not quite so dark but still beautiful, quite spectacular in truth, framed with those outrageously lavish long black lashes. He still took her breath away.

Lexy examined her beautifully cooked omelette and toast and tea and grinned. 'I'm sensing that that expression "high maintenance" rankled last night. You do know that I've never had breakfast served to me in bed in my entire life?'

Nic frowned and sank down on the side of the bed beside her. 'Surely for a treat when you were a child at least?'

Lexy shook her head. 'Not once. If you weren't at the table on the dot of the hour, you didn't eat.'

'Sounds like I'm likely to be spoiling you rotten,' Nic said wryly of that strict childhood regime.

Lexy laughed as she tucked into her excellent omelette. 'You're not likely to get any objections from me.'

It was only as she finished actually eating and sipped her tea that she removed her mesmerised gaze from Nic and noticed that the snow had vanished from the trees outside. They were no longer white skeletons of winter trees clad in snow. 'The snow stopped, I see,' she muttered in surprise.

'Yes, it started raining in the middle of the night and it's mostly gone now.'

Pushing away the tray, she snatched up his discarded tee shirt again even though her brain told her that it was silly to be that modest with a guy she had spent the whole night in bed with. Cheeks pink, she emerged from its enveloping folds, catching the amusement in his gaze and lifting her chin in defiance of it because she couldn't change her inclinations in the matter of a few hours of an intimacy that was entirely new to her. She scrambled out of bed to stand at the tall windows and in the distance she could see the black ribbon of the road, clear of snow. In reality, her heart sank at that view because she knew she wanted to stay with him for the rest of the weekend, but she also knew that she could *not* stay.

'Can you drop me at the nearest railway station?' she asked him uncomfortably.

'Why on earth would I do that? I assumed you were staying on here with me,' he intoned tautly.

'I'm sorry. I would love to, but I can't. I've got to be in London by tonight because I'm being picked up very early to attend a christening tomorrow in Cornwall.'

'I'm sure your friends will understand that the vagaries of the weather have intervened,' Nic countered drily.

Lexy spun back to him, read the tension in his lean, darkly handsome face and almost bottled out. 'No, they won't. I've been chosen as a godmother and I agreed,' she pushed herself to declare.

'Is this for a very close friend?'

'I don't think that comes into it.' Lexy squared her slight shoulders and gazed back at him with a faint hint of reproach in her bearing. 'I said I'd do it and just because it doesn't suit me quite so much now isn't an excuse to let them down.'

His ebony brows flared. 'You didn't know that

you would be stuck in the wilds of Yorkshire when you agreed.'

'A reasonable point, but I'm not stuck any more. I can see the road and it's clear.' Lexy could feel his annoyance and frustration with her and the irony was that she would have given almost anything to cave in and say that she would stay and forget her christening obligation. 'But the truth is that when I make a promise, I keep it and I don't let people down at the last minute. And, Nic? That's not a bad trait to have, so don't make me feel bad about it.'

'I'm not trying to do...hell, pack up and I'll get the car warmed up,' he breathed curtly and she could literally see him accepting her argument and stifling his disappointment for her benefit and she relaxed again, as much as she was capable of relaxing when she was going against her own nature.

Clad in his tee shirt, she gathered up her discarded clothes in the room next door and hurried back downstairs to shower and pack as quickly as she could manage it. Was she crazy? she asked herself as she dried her hair. To leave a man whom she had just met but who had become outrageously important to her within a few hours? But that was life and if he wasn't interested in an ongoing relationship of any kind, staying on with him for one more day and night wouldn't be a guarantee either, she reminded herself doggedly. Either he was interested or he wasn't: it was that simple.

As she arrived back in the hall with her case and bag, Nic stepped forward, his overcoat and boots on now. 'You don't even have a coat!'

'It's still in the hire car,' she recalled belatedly.

'We'll stop on the way. I'm sure the car will still be there,' he said grimly.

'I can't ask you.'

'You're not asking. I'm telling you that you're not leaving in weather like this *without* a coat,' Nic told her fiercely as he opened the front door.

She felt as though a lifetime had passed since she last climbed into his SUV. This time she was noticing that it was the very last word in opulence. She breathed in deep and slow to steady herself. 'I really am sorry that I have to leave.'

'My number is in your phone,' he told her, sharply disconcerting her. 'I put it in last night. What are you thinking of, not even having a password on your phone? I was so surprised that it opened for me that I just went ahead and added myself to your contacts.'

'That's okay.' Lexy bent her head but she was smiling like mad below her tumbling hair as he parked the car on the verge. Seconds later, she watched him break through the hedge and stride with innate impatience across the still snow-covered field towards the car she had crashed.

She wasn't falling for him, she assured herself, because nobody fell in love in a matter of eighteen hours, nobody normal or sensible anyway. It was just that she liked him, liked him an awful lot, she reasoned, and it wasn't only the sex, although that had been pretty spectacular. He was clever, he was kind, he was thoughtful and even though she suspected that it would come naturally to him to rap out orders like a domineering boss, he was controlling that tendency for her benefit. She laughed at herself as he reappeared at her side of the car and got her out to help her into her sensible winter coat. A full-bodied shiver ran through her as he carefully tugged her hair out from below the collar. He had yet to show her one thing about himself that she didn't like or appreciate.

He insisted on driving her all the way into Manchester, paid for the ticket when they arrived and he stayed with her until it was time for her to leave him. When he buttoned up her coat for her as though she were a child before she went through the barrier onto the platform, her eyes prickled with tears because nobody had taken that much care of her in more years than she cared to count. Armed with enough magazines to take on a world tour, she got on the train, still struggling to catch a last view of him, still struggling to credit that the whole encounter had not been some insane, wondrous dream…

Eighteen months later

Nic strode into his lawyer's office. Aubrey Harrison, a thin, sharp-featured man in his thirties, sprang upright to greet him.

'Sorry about this,' he said wryly. 'But I thought you should look at this paternity claim before it goes down the inevitable DNA route. It's a rather odd one.'

'Not another one,' Nic groaned in exasperation, because it seemed that no matter how careful he was, the false claims still came in.

Yet in years he had never had anything more than a one-night stand or, at most, a couple of nights with a woman. Obviously, he knew that accidental conception could occur and that such matters had to be checked out, but even so, they put him in a bad mood, regardless of how hard he tried to take them in his stride. It wasn't as though he had ever been a real playboy like his older brother, Jace. And in recent times, he pondered, his innate reserve locking down his lean, hard bone structure, there had been no play time included in his driven schedule. He had always been more into work than casual sex and only one woman had ever bucked that trend with him. As for her, she was long gone, lost in the wind along with her phone number.

Yes, he had made an elementary mistake and paid for it. Her number had simply vanished from his phone as though it had never been and at the same time as he had tried to check that mystery out, he had found a suspicious app on his phone that was tracking his calls and texts. That and the security concerns aroused by it had proved a major headache, he recalled grimly. Even so, in spite of the investigation he had had done, he had yet to discover the culprit.

'This claimant seems fanciful at the very least and the timing is all off. Why would she wait *this* long to claim child support?' Aubrey wondered, passing a document to Nic.

Nic took one cursory glance at the name and froze, not a muscle moving on his taut dark features while disbelief assailed him in a blinding surge. 'Lexy…' he almost whispered. Lexy Montgomery. Now that surname would have been very welcome had he known it, had he even thought to *ask* for it eighteen months earlier, only he hadn't. And he had had no success trying to find a Korean interpreter called Lexy in London.

'I take it that you actually know this woman,' Aubrey remarked in some surprise.

'Yes.' Nic had to clear his throat before he could speak. 'I know her but a lot of time has passed since we were together.'

'Our investigator wasn't able to discover a link between you and Miss Montgomery and she has no social media, which is strange in this day and age.'

Shaking his head as though to clear it, Nic forced his attention back to the document in his hold. 'There are *three* children,' he registered on an incredulous note.

'Triplets. Two boys and a girl. Even more unlikely, I surmised. The stats say only one in ten thousand births is a triplet one,' the lawyer maintained. 'And the chances of having triplets by a chance-met billionaire in the tech industry have to be even poorer.'

Nic was pale below his golden skin. 'My mother's mother was a triplet, one of three girls, and my mother is a twin. There have also been multiple births on my father's side of the family tree. It's not as unusual as you might think,' he commented flatly, thinking of how downright irresponsible he had been with Lexy that night and of how very possible it would be for her to have fallen pregnant. Guilt engulfed him in a crashing wave.

'What I don't understand is why she didn't phone me, when she had my number,' he confessed out loud.

'According to her solicitor innumerable efforts were made to contact you in person and by letter and phone and all of them failed. How do you want to proceed with this?'

Nic vaulted upright. 'I want to see her,' he said instantaneously.

'That's not on the table, Nic, and I would strongly advise you not to think along those lines before a DNA test establishes that these children are yours.'

'I'll do the DNA test immediately, but I'm more interested in knowing where she's living.'

'The information given is not current. I checked that out,' his lawyer informed him.

Resolving to find that out now that he was armed with Lexy's full name, Nic departed. Three babies, he found himself thinking in astonishment. Was that possible? He knew it was possible from his own family tree and he also knew that he had been reckless with her, reckless with a woman for the first time in his life, he reminded himself. But why hadn't she contacted him? Got pushy if she ran into some little difficulties? He couldn't imagine Lexy being pushy, didn't think she was the type. Not that she lacked backbone, he reasoned, just that she was sort of soft, gentle, not aggressive by nature and he had liked that about her, only not if that lack in her had kept them apart for more than eighteen months. While pondering that he was also working out how to get her address and a background report.

'It's the perfect night for a barbecue,' Angeliki declared, strolling into his office later that day as he sat at his desk, having been determined to work and put Lexy and the three babies he *might* suddenly have totally out of his mind. Only that hadn't worked. Two boys and a girl, born only seven months after that night, which meant that something had gone wrong with the pregnancy and the whole lot of them might have died. That horrified him and knocked him straight back into abstraction.

'I'm afraid I'm not in the mood,' Nic admitted, forcing a smile for her benefit. 'Sorry.'

Their estrangement hadn't lasted for long, he recalled. Angeliki had phoned and then come to see him. She had confessed that the breakdown of yet another of her fleeting relationships and a sense of insecurity had prompted her into that inadvisable straying into his bed. Of course, he had forgiven her, but he still hadn't told her that she was his half-sister, even though he had told his brother. And Jace? Jace had merely rolled his eyes without much perceptible interest in the news that he had a sister. Why? Probably because Jace was already dug deep into playing happy families with his wife, Gigi, and his little son, Nikolaos. A reformed rake, Jace was so into Gigi and their progeny that Nic was wholly glad to be heart whole and still fancy-free.

Nic, however, was feeling guilty that he still hadn't told anyone else, but he couldn't see that being given the news that she was a secret Diamandis would decrease Angeliki's general discontentment with life. Angeliki was an heiress because his father had made provision for her long ago, only that wealth, supposedly inherited from a distant relative, hadn't made her any happier. And unfortunately, she was still very much given to referring to that night Nic had rejected her, instead of just leaving that controversial topic alone, even though she had to see that it still made him uncomfortable to think of her in naked, seductive mode.

'You're not much fun today.' Heaving a sigh, Angeliki batted her eyelashes at him in annoyance as she leant back against his desk. 'What about tomorrow night?'

'I'm dealing with a bit of a crisis right now,' Nic told her with perfect truth.

'You should've said that first!' the beautiful blonde exclaimed in reproof. 'You can be so secretive about things that it worries me. Are you still seeing Mila Jetson?'

Nic shrugged. 'No, that's over.'

He recognised that he no longer confided in his friend as he once had but, having only recently registered her response to the women who passed through his life when Mila had complained, he wasn't unleashing her on the likes of Lexy. Angeliki could be bitchy and critical and very devious, and Lexy was none of those things, although if those babies were his, and he had to assume within the time frame that they *were*, she had some explaining to do about why she hadn't made tracking him down her priority months ago. He was angry about that. He was *very* angry about that omission, he reminded himself, and it took a great deal to make Nic angry.

'Good news, I hope,' Lexy's solicitor passed on during her first call in weeks. 'Mr Diamandis has already lodged his DNA sample with a private firm and has requested permission to send one of their lab techs out to your home to speed up this process.'

'My goodness…' Lexy murmured in genuine astonishment.

'I suspect he's keen to deal quickly and quietly with the claim. Will you agree to me passing on your address and phone number for the collection of your sample?'

'Of course.' Lexy knew she didn't have much choice and would be grateful to avoid the stress and expense of a trip out. She hadn't worked full-time since she was five months pregnant. Eileen sent her occasional bits of translation work and she put the triplets in daycare one day a week to accomplish it. As she was living with the help of welfare, she received some free childcare, but nothing she was allowed to earn part-time in such circumstances was up to the challenge of keeping a decent roof over their heads.

That was why, as she moved back into the spacious living room to rejoin her friend Mel and share the contents of that call, she was beaming, because their current home was only a temporary one. She was house-sitting for Mel's parents while her father took up a year's placement on the faculty of a New York college. She looked after the family pets, Barney the Labrador and Chica the cat, and the house plants, keeping the lawn cut and the dust down. In return she received the use of their car and the glorious relief of having a comfortable place to live. But time was running out because the Fosters would be returning home in another few weeks and she would soon be homeless *again.*

'About time he stepped up to do something other than ignoring you!' Mel, a tall, lanky brunette exclaimed. 'Stop acting like your boat's finally come in. This is only his first move and, of course, he'll still be hoping the kids aren't *his* right now.'

Lexy compressed her lips. 'Well, I'm choosing to hope that he's finally come to his senses and accepted that he can't avoid his responsibilities any longer. I just wish I'd listened to you and gone straight to a solicitor as soon as they were born. I've wasted so much time with my phone calls and my letters and visits to that wretched office block of his. He truly is the most hateful man.'

Mel glanced at her watch and stood up. 'I'll have to run if I'm hoping to make dinner with Fergus tonight,' she confided. 'Sorry I can't stay longer.'

Lexy hugged her best friend with a lump in her throat because without that friendship, she honestly wasn't sure she could have made it through the horrendous challenges she had faced over the past eighteen months. Mel had been solid gold right from the start. She had never uttered a word of criticism over Lexy's very bad decision to spend the night with a gorgeous stranger. Nor had she said anything while, with hindsight, Lexy had waited with such foolish confidence for Nic Diamandis to phone her afterwards and had never heard from him again. And when Lexy had needed support and understanding, Mel had been there for her every time.

She went upstairs to lift her children from their nap. *Children!* Even when she wasn't consumed with worry about the future, she still marvelled at the wonder of her three babies. Ethan was already standing in his cot awaiting her arrival, which was par for the course. Ezra, his smaller twin, whose former health problems had meant his survival had been touch and go for a while, was lying back, eyes open but quite relaxed as usual. If Ethan was the boisterous one, Ezra was the quiet, more thoughtful one. And last, but far from being least, came her daughter, Lily, bouncing at the side of the cot in readiness to be lifted.

She grabbed two of them up and hurtled downstairs to place them in the playpen before returning to lift Ezra. He beamed up at her and she cuddled him. It struck her as particularly ironic that not one of her children looked remotely like her. They were a trio with unruly black hair, dark eyes and olive skin.

A call came from the DNA lab that afternoon and she agreed to a lab tech calling with her because it would save her a lot of hassle. Transporting three babies anywhere, even with the use of a car, was exhausting. The tech arrived within an hour of the phone call, which disconcerted her because she had expected to have to wait in at least the next day for the visit. The woman was barely in the house for ten minutes, taking a mouth swab with the minimum of fuss and promising speedy results. Lexy was tempted to say that she was in no doubt of what the results would be, but she said nothing.

She assumed that the triplets' father would be praying that the results were not a match. After all, he had gone to some trouble to avoid ever seeing her again. She had been informed that her phone calls to his office were unwelcome and once she had even been escorted back onto the street by two very embarrassed and apologetic security guards. Slowly but surely her mortification had become burnished by wounded pride and rage at the level his behaviour had reduced her dignity to. She owed Nic Diamandis nothing. However, she had become ever more determined that he should help to support his own children. She wanted nothing else from him and sincerely hoped that she would never have to actually lay eyes on him again.

That hope was plunged into disappointment two days later when the doorbell rang. Lexy was unprepared for a shock. It was her work day, and her children were at the nursery. She was clad in yoga pants and a tank top, spectacles firmly anchored on her nose and wearing not a scrap of make-up when she went to answer the door, expecting the postman. Only instead she found herself focusing in disbelief on the man she had spent months trying to see or contact, firmly, squarely planted on her doorstep. And she couldn't *believe* that Nic Diamandis was finally giving her the time of day, not after all her failed efforts and his established ghosting of her very existence.

'Nic…' Her greeting was weak and it swiftly died away, along with her voice.

'Lexy. We need to talk.'

Lexy tilted her chin. 'A bit late in the day for that, isn't it?' she heard herself quip, incredulity and bitter anger consuming her as he gazed back at her with apparently not even an ounce of decent discomfort.

And without another word, Lexy slammed the door shut in his face again, steaming with the recollection of all the many humiliations he had had heaped on her when he had evidently blocked her calls on the number he had given her and had then refused to recognise her name when she'd tried to see him, or even *speak* to him, at his precious giant office building in the city of London. No, no regrets, she reflected as she paced away from the door again, her arms folded in a defensive block. What sort of father figure would he be for her children anyway? There was no way that she would allow him to treat her kids the way her father had treated her, making her feel less, making her feel unwanted even within her own home.

Been there, done that, got the lesson in triplicate, not falling for the act again…*ever*!

CHAPTER FOUR

'YOU'VE GOT A huge problem here,' Jace Diamandis mused as he strolled across his sunlit office. 'No offence, but you've really screwed this up.'

'You think I don't know that?' Nic slung back at his older brother in a temper. 'Lexy has my kids and I doubt that she'll even let me see them!'

'Is it these kids or her you're really into?' Jace enquired lazily, watching his brother pace back and forth like a tiger in a too small cage.

'I can't be into children I've never even met,' Nic intoned grittily. 'But I *was* into her... Well, I was until she slammed that door in my face.'

'Nothing like an angry woman to knock you back to earth,' Jace opined unhelpfully, making Nic wonder why he had approached his elder brother for advice. 'But if you want to ace this, you're going to have to borrow a trait or two from our dear old, unlamented dad, Argus.'

Nic shot back a question for clarity in guttural Greek.

'You've got no rights as an unmarried father under British law. If she says it's detrimental to their interests to be in contact with you, her vote as their mother counts more than yours. What the hell did you do to her to make her that hostile?'

'I haven't *done* anything!' Nic proclaimed with pride.

'Doesn't sound like it,' Jace remarked gently. 'But if you want access to those babies, you're bound to bring in the big guns. It's your duty as their father. You need to marry her and then you'll have rights.'

Marriage! The concept was like a punch in the gut to Nic.

'Our father didn't think that way,' Nic breathed stiffly, striving not to feel uncomfortable about the reality that his path into the Diamandis family had not been as smooth or, indeed, as pristine as Jace's. He was the son of the mistress, raised in status only after his father was widowed and had rejected his firstborn son. He had always felt a little like a consolation prize, only brought into his father's public life to ease the stinging humiliation of an unfaithful first wife. And he knew that his mother, Bianca, had always felt the same…like an afterthought, a pretender to the Diamandis throne.

'No, but, sad to say, threats and intimidation work and you may need them to access those children.'

'I'm not that kind of man.'

'Just saying. Clean and upfront may not work but it *is* your job to bring those babies into our family, however low you may have to sink to achieve that,' Jace completed without apology. 'I'll put my legal team on it for you.'

'I have a lawyer of my own,' Nic protested.

'You need the big guns now,' his brother asserted. 'And family is family, Nic.'

'You certainly don't view Angeliki in that light,' Nic commented.

Jace grimaced. 'Our half-sister has an unpleasant reputation and she's not the nicest woman around. I'm in no hurry to claim her and that's why. How you can count her as a close friend escapes me. I know you grew up together but—'

'Nobody's twisting your arm to acknowledge her,' Nic broke in with the loyalty that was innate in him. 'But she's honestly not as mean as you seem to think or I wouldn't spend any time with her.'

Jace laughed. 'Because she plays nice with you. I suspect she still has plans to get you to the altar and you're the guy that *still* won't tell her what she needs to know to back off!'

Exasperated by his brother's sense of humour, Nic went to see his lawyer, Aubrey, only to discover that the Diamandis legal team had already been in touch with advice, none of which Nic wished to follow. Yes, he could play hardball with the best of them but not with the mother of his children, he reasoned grimly.

Coming to see you around eleven.

That was what the text announced at eight a.m.

Lexy worked through a mess of emotional reactions. No, she didn't owe Nic Diamandis the time of day but, at the same time, he was the father of her kids and simply ignoring him as he had long ignored her wasn't a good idea. Sooner or later, the triplets would inevitably decide that *they* wanted to know him. What was so very attractive about a billionaire? Well, inevitable was the exact right word, she had decided. He would be in a position to offer adventurous days out that were only a dream on her horizon. She couldn't shut him out of their lives, even if she wanted to in retribution. He *deserved* to be shut out of their lives but possibly his children would have a very different take on that outlook.

So, because he was like an inescapable blight on all their lives, she would accept *one* visit. She would let him satisfy his curiosity. And hopefully that would be the end of the whole drama. What single, very good-looking billionaire wanted to settle down to having triplet babies on the regular? She was safe. The first messy nappy would see him off, or a spit up or a meltdown. She had seen him on the Internet, with gorgeous, unattainable women clinging to his flawlessly groomed arm like magnets, the most recent a supermodel with the brain of a very tiny bird—proved by the telling interview she had given—but the body and face of a woman so perfect she looked unattainable to ordinary females. Lexy had only qualified for attention because she had been the only option available on a snowy night in the depths of Yorkshire. A man of Nic's ilk didn't do babies in the raw and there was nothing rawer than babies, wild and untrammelled and totally unpredictable as they could be.

Nic arrived, well primed for the challenge of babies, for young children had never been on his radar. His brother, however, was an experienced hand, able to fully convey the potential horrors that had enabled Nic to look now at any baby in much the way he might have regarded an unexploded bomb.

Lexy opened the door, confident in the conviction that she was decently dressed this time around.

Nic took one glance at the narrow skirt and shirt and suppressed a sigh. On his last very brief visit, he had never seen anything sexier than the yoga pants and the spectacles on Lexy with her hair all tousled and impossibly sexy, just the way it had looked when she'd got out of his bed following a night he had never forgotten. And then she'd spun round, her exquisite face out of view, to give him a glimpse of how she looked from behind and that fast the yoga pants had vanished from his memory as he'd measured instead the perfection of her slender hips and surprisingly plump derrière in the fine fabric. He had breathed in deep and slow, striving to stave off the swell in his groin, genuinely embarrassed by his own reaction because, *Thee mou*, he wasn't a teenager any more when such responses were inevitable.

Lexy was priding herself on her essential decency.

She could have let the babies get overtired and treated him to their worst but instead she had let them have that early morning nap as usual and get up again, once more restored to good humour. The trio of babies on the rug all looked up as she reappeared and they, every one of them, smiled. She supposed it was just as well that her kids had no idea whatsoever that their foolish mother had just been slaughtered in the mental stakes by their father. Truth was, Nic was still impossibly pretty. She had rationalised him in photos online, reduced his appeal, fought off the effect of his sexy sizzle.

Only all of that didn't work in the flesh. Here he was in person, as flamboyantly gorgeous as a tropical sunset and raining all over her parade of indifference. Black designer jeans outlining every powerful line of his narrow waist, lean hips and long, strong legs, a simple tee shirt framing what had to be the muscular chest definition of a pin-up. He was a study in raw masculinity and sensuality.

She wished that Mel were there to bring her down to earth again with a necessary bump and remind her that Nic Diamandis might look like a dream in face and body, but in character he was the very definition of a rat or some far less presentable word. He wasn't the man she had believed he was the night they had first met. She had been naïve, and he had been deceptive in everything he said and did with her.

'So, here they are. The reason I assume that you

were so keen to come here in person and finally acknowledge my existence,' Lexy remarked brittly, unable to resist inserting that last little provocative reminder.

Nic stared down at a rug containing a virtual scrum of babies. The littlest one gave him a huge smile and, that fast, Nic was dropping down on his knees to try and reach their level and not be scary to them. The little one crawled on hands and knees straight over to him with the most charming air of acceptance and clambered up onto his lap.

'And this is…?' He had been meaning to pick Lexy up about that crack about his failing to acknowledge her existence, but the approaching baby had trumped that urge.

'Ezra. That's Ezra.' In truth, Lexy was disconcerted by Ezra's attitude because he was usually the wariest of her trio. 'Ethan's twin.'

'Why's he so much smaller than his twin?' Nic asked straight off.

'He wasn't thriving in the womb like Ethan and Lily, which is why they all had to be delivered early, and initially he had breathing problems,' Lexy confided reluctantly. 'But he's slowly catching up by growing faster than his big brother.'

'So kind of you to keep me informed,' Nic voiced between gritted teeth while smiling because Ethan, the larger twin, was coming his way, but his daughter, Lily, was still staring, undecided, from the other side of the rug.

'I made every possible effort under the sun to keep you informed but I met with a blank brick wall,' Lexy framed very politely.

'You're lying and you know you are,' Nic murmured softly.

And that fast, in the wake of that toxic exchange, Lexy wanted to kill him stone dead, all her recollections of being pregnant and alone and a mother and alone piling up inside her like a threatening avalanche. 'I hate you,' she said equally softly. 'I hate you so much I can't stand having you here but I'm trying very hard indeed to be civilised.'

'Civilised is not always what it appears to be,' Nic quipped as Ethan clambered onto his lap, trying to stand up, failing, trying again, grabbing at Nic's hands to show him how to play the game he wanted. Reminded of Jace and his indomitable spirit, Nic smiled down at his son and let him jump up and down happily with the support of his hands. *This*, he decided, was what was truly important, *not* her and her poor attitude.

Lily was sidling closer to him, big brown eyes fixed to him as though he might bite and, in her, he saw her mother, more anxious, more scared than any Diamandis had ever been, and it annoyed him. His daughter was afraid of him and that *was* unmistakeably Lexy's fault.

He freed Ethan to the toy that was stealing his attention and reached for Lily. She came to him with huge, troubled eyes and he judged Lexy even harder for that distrust. On his lap, she settled and kept on gazing up at him with a growing steadiness that entranced his cynical soul. Then, without the smallest warning, she clawed her way up the front of his tee shirt and wrapped both arms round him. It was unexpected but very welcome and he hugged her close with gratitude that she was still sufficiently trusting to offer a stranger that affection. Even so, Lexy's outright hostility took him aback. Why was she lying to him? She hadn't got in touch with him, indeed hadn't made the smallest attempt to contact him.

Tense silence reigned while Nic engaged the babies with the toys on the rug. Lexy could feel her own face growing stiffer and stiffer because she was so angry with him and she couldn't express it.

'Would you like coffee?' she asked curtly.

'No, thank you. I won't be staying much longer,' Nic murmured flatly.

'Good. I have to give them lunch soon and that's a very messy deal,' she declared, striving to lighten the atmosphere a little for the sake of good manners.

Lexy could not recognise the man in front of her as the man she had met and shared a bed with, which she supposed was her warning that she had mistaken his character from the outset. He was cool and guarded and irredeemably superior, very much a posh, sophisticated Diamandis male. He hadn't been any of that when they had met, not even at first and not later either, she recalled with lingering pain.

'We could leave the kitchen door open and have a word in there,' she proffered, very keen to ensure that he did not have an excuse to make a second visit.

Nic vaulted upright with easy athletic grace and scanned her where she stood in the doorway. 'Whose house is this?' he asked.

'My best friend, Mel's parents own it,' Lexy divulged reluctantly. 'They're abroad. I'm the housesitter. I look after their pets, plants and try to keep the lawn down.'

'You don't rent or own it, then. You have a home elsewhere?'

Lexy was wondering why he was being so nosy. 'No, I don't. Between having three young children and being unable to work full-time for more than a year now, my options are few.'

'You're virtually homeless,' Nic informed her, as if she mightn't already have grasped that fact.

'And that could be because the father of my children has paid nothing whatsoever towards their support!' Lexy fired back at him without hesitation.

'Skase!' Nic shot down at her, because she had almost shouted that response.

'And what does that command mean in English?'

'Keep quiet,' Nic translated the politer term frigidly, because all he could see was the three babies who had crawled over to join them, all three faces raised and brimming with curiosity and possibly even a little annoyance that they had been abandoned as the centre of attention. He scolded himself for that fanciful thought, not even convinced that babies that young had much in the way of thought.

And then to his horror all three faces crumpled and they burst into tears. Lexy brushed past him and got down on the floor to comfort them and they swarmed her like little vultures, nestling, clutching, grabbing, howling.

'It's *my* fault. I raised my voice to you and it frightened them,' Lexy framed as the howling subsided to more manageable levels.

'I'll leave you to feed them,' Nic said levelly. 'I'll come back tonight at eight and we'll talk then.'

'Fight, you mean.'

'I have no intention of fighting with you,' Nic asserted with glacial bite. 'You are the mother of my children and I respect that status even if I'm a little dubious about you as a person.'

'Thanks, but no, thanks,' Lexy muttered as he vanished out of the front door and she shut it firmly behind him.

'Well, how did it go?' Mel demanded on the phone an hour later.

'Not very well. We argued through it as best we could with the triplets there and he's coming back this evening to argue some more. Nic really doesn't like being told that he fell down on his responsibilities.'

'And that's catnip for you at the minute,' her friend guessed. 'But maybe give the aggro a rest until you can get some kind of adult arrangement ironed out between you.'

'I was hoping he would just pay up and go away.'

'I don't think you know him well enough to decide how he may react to being a father,' Mel countered with tact.

Unwelcome though they were, Mel's shrewd comments cooled Lexy's anger with Nic. Did she really want to drive him away so totally that her babies lost out on the possibility of a father figure? And the answer to that was…no, she didn't. In other words, she couldn't afford to be short-sighted. Literally and figuratively, she reflected wryly as she studied her little trio striving to feed themselves and dropping food everywhere round their battered mismatched highchairs. If Nic was capable of loving her babies, his interest in them would be invaluable.

Right now, Lexy was broke, totally broke, and it was like that every week, stretching the pennies to go further, adding up the groceries at the supermarket before she went to pay, getting in first at the charity shop to search the rails. She was poor, she was so poor she had given up make-up and all sorts of stuff she had once naively taken for granted. And that was the world she lived in when her kids deserved so much better from their rich father. If he could offer more, then it was her duty to accept it and be polite about it. Taking potshots at him wasn't going to fill the kitty or put food on the table.

Unaware of Lexy's resolve to be less incendiary, Nic was brooding. He was angry, so angry with her for subjecting them both and their children to what promised to be chaos and bad publicity. But for all he knew, Lexy would enjoy that kind of attention because she wasn't the woman he remembered. Yes, she was still attractive to him to the most annoying degree but everything that he had admired inside her seemed to have vanished. There was nothing sweet or gentle about that waspish tongue of hers or the angry dislike flashing in her eyes.

In truth, Nic had never dealt with an angry woman in his life. Jace had seemed much more seasoned in that line. Nic had handled Angeliki's angry flouncing and dirty glares but she had never got verbal with him or insulted him and he did not think their friendship would have survived had she done so. Why? Nic had a low threshold for insults because he reckoned that every day from birth until his demise, his father, Argus, had hurt, humiliated or outraged him in some way. Even adult status hadn't protected him. Argus had liked to get on the phone to critique his business choices, his performance, his choice of friends. In fact, Argus had been his horrible abusive self, right up until the very day he died. To both Nic *and* his unhappy, derided mother.

Lexy had to change before Nic's second visit. A dressy shirt did not long survive triplet proximity. She didn't have many clothes. When she was pregnant, she had traded in good stuff in return for anything that could fit a small woman with a physically large pregnant belly. All she had left were the items nobody had wanted and she knew it was time to get on with the lawn again, a never-ending duty in summer time, so on went her denim shorts and a tee. Probably the same tee he had once taken *off* her all too willing body, she reflected morosely as she brushed her hair and left it loose.

The ride-on mower was an unpredictable horror that didn't always work and visits from the local mechanic were a regular feature. As soon as the triplets were down, she went out to tackle the mower and when, glory of glories, it worked, nothing would have removed her bottom from that seat until she had done the whole lawn. She was near the end of the back lawn when she saw Nic standing below the rear porch watching her and looking a bit like the Grim Reaper in a dark suit, faithfully cut to make the most of every line and muscle in his long, lean physique. He looked maddeningly stupendous, and she was stricken that she had lost sight of time and hadn't contrived to get indoors again and change into something more appropriate for his benefit. Even so, mindful of her new attitude, she lifted her hand in as friendly a wave of acknowledgement as she could fake and pointed at the corner to let him know she would be stopping when she finished the grass. One last strip to go.

The ear-splitting decibels of the mower stopped and Lexy removed the headphones she had been using and manoeuvred off the machine with all the awkwardness of her unfortunately short legs. Tugging self-consciously at the hem of the denim shorts, she hurried up the slope and onto the rear patio to greet him.

'I'm sorry to have kept you waiting but once I get the mower going, I stay on it until I'm finished,' she confided, anxiously fixing her gaze on his lean, strong, utterly expressionless face.

'Why are you not angry any more?' Nic enquired disconcertingly.

Lexy grimaced, feeling more uncomfortable than ever as she led the way indoors through the kitchen into the living room. 'It's not that I'm not angry, just that anger isn't a good idea right now with you only just meeting the triplets. I need to stop letting it get in the way,' she muttered.

Nic was astonished that she had done exactly what he had been hoping she would do to ponder and reach the same conclusions he had. There was no profit in an angry resentment that kept them at daggers drawn.

Together they were parents to three children and the children were what mattered most.

'Coffee? A drink?' Lexy proffered.

Nic was studying her legs, very shapely legs, he had to admit. 'Coffee…black, no sugar.'

'I remember.'

'The less we remember now from our first meeting, the better,' Nic startled her by proclaiming. 'The situation has changed radically and time has moved on without…well, without me. I want to correct that.'

'And how do you think it best to do that?' Lexy called out from the kitchen as she poured the coffee she had brewed in readiness, grateful that the larder was so well stocked, although she had rarely used anything from her hosts' cupboards for the food was not hers.

'I think we should get married,' Nic drawled, almost in a chatty tone, as if what he was saying were not anything like as shocking as it was.

'I beg your pardon?' she murmured, the hand holding the jug shaking.

Nic sprang upright and walked back to the doorway to look at her with grave dark brown eyes. 'Marriage will fix everything—'

'Nothing's broken,' she just about whispered in her disbelief.

'It is in my world,' Nic contradicted. 'My children are illegitimate, which will very much upset my whole family and make it almost impossible for them to inherit anything from us. I owe them *and* you more than some paltry monthly payment towards their support. You're homeless and penniless and none of you should be living like that. If we were to marry, you would all be properly taken care of.'

'Maybe I don't need to be taken care of,' Lexy framed, cheeks hot with shame from being called 'homeless and penniless' in one sentence, even if it was true.

Staring down at her, Nic was reading everything in her aquamarine eyes. Mortification, resentment, hurt. It shook him inside out to see those feelings in her face because it knocked him right back to their one and only night together. 'Everyone needs taking care of occasionally,' he pointed out.

Lexy winced and passed him his coffee. 'You don't understand. I've been living on handouts and other people's kindness since even before the babies were born,' she admitted chokily. 'My friend Mel and her parents have been unbelievably good to me.'

'If you marry me, you'll never have to worry about money or where you live ever again,' Nic murmured like a snake charmer.

Lexy vented a choking laugh that was a partial sob because she was fighting to hold the tears back. The very last thing she had expected from Nic Diamandis was a marriage proposal. It was so old-fashioned, so wildly unexpected from the man who had ignored her and their babies' needs while it evidently had suited him to do so. 'I'm not sure I can believe that you are sincere with this…or that you could suggest that I marry you for your money,' she muttered. 'I mean, I would never ever even consider marrying a man for his money. I'm not a gold-digger or a—'

Nic caught one of the hands she was waving dismissively in the air between them and held it to steady her. She was all over the place, like a tree rocking in a storm, and he could see the tears glimmering in her beautiful eyes. He hadn't intended to upset her. He had intended to soothe her, offer her options, and marriage had not been his first choice of those options, even if it was only matrimony that would satisfy his family, end the drama and give him unalienable rights over their three children.

'I would be happy for you to marry me for my wealth.'

'But clearly you're not talking about a n-normal marriage,' she stammered, sneaking a questioning look up at him.

'A marriage on paper, obviously,' he conceded, while striving not to notice the pert shimmy of her clearly unbound breasts below the tee shirt and monitor his own very, very hungry body. She was dynamite in a tiny package, his personal kryptonite, it seemed. 'But you'd have to fake being a real bride for my family's benefit because that will integrate our triplets into the group and make everything smooth again.'

Lexy's lower lip had long since parted with the upper as sheer disbelief gripped her hard. 'So, you're serious about this marriage idea. It seems like you've thought it through and you like things…er, smooth.'

'Call it crisis management. It's my strength,' Nic told her in a very businesslike tone. 'We marry for a while. You acquire a proper home, in this country or wherever else you wish to live. The children get to know their father. All the complications melt away. When we have had enough of the pretence we go for a divorce and co-parent.'

Marry *for a while*. That put the proposal in a much clearer perspective, she acknowledged ruefully. It would be a temporary arrangement, not the usual life commitment. And she could see his point. Like whitewashing a dirty wall, the end result would be very visible. She and her children would have recognised importance in his world and evidently that meant a lot to Nic Diamandis. As a wife or even an ex-wife, she would have a position and nobody would pity her or look down on her. Their children would be recognised as family members while all her money worries would go away.

'Why are you willing to do this? I mean…it's more of a big thing for you with your lifestyle than it would be for me,' Lexy pointed out with as much tact as she could employ, because a playboy faking a marriage could hardly engage in his normal pursuits. Unless, of course, and again she was being naïve, his cheating outside marriage could provide the reason for an eventual divorce? She decided not to ask any more awkward questions and was beginning to turn away.

'I'm willing to do it because my mother was my father's mistress before he married her. A *married* man's mistress.' Nic spelt out that reluctant admission between compressed lips and Lexy stopped dead in her tracks. 'I was three years old before my father married my mother after he was widowed by an unfaithful wife. Pulling us forward into his life officially was a face-saving gesture, no more.'

Lexy slowly turned back, cut to the bone by that sudden unexpected confession that sliced away all that Diamandis gloss and revealed the truth of the ordinary humans behind the billionaire façade. 'Oh...' was all she felt able to say about such a very personal and private thing.

Nic expelled his breath in a sharp exhalation. 'And all the years I was growing up I felt that my mother and I were looked down on within the family as being something less than his first wife and my elder brother. I don't want that happening to my children.'

Lexy nodded jerkily, finally fully understanding that motivation and trying not to be touched that he had confided in her. After all, that motive was absolutely understandable in his position, considering his own more humble beginnings. Nic hadn't started out as a Diamandis with a silver spoon in his mouth. No, he had been the son of his father's lover on the side and disregarded while his father was still married to another woman. That knowledge shook her rigid, taught her afresh that appearances were often misleading and that she too had judged Nic to be an absolute four-letter word of a man because of his privilege in life and his treatment of her.

For the first time, as well, it occurred to her that his treatment of her did not line up with the man wishing to marry her to prevent his children from enduring that sense of insecurity that he had suffered as a young boy. He was more sensitive than she had appreciated, under that surface gloss, that flaring, oh, so attractive confidence.

Amazingly, it took very little thought at all for her to decide that, yes, now that he had talked the talk, she would give him her trust and marry him. Ethan, Ezra and Lily would profit from that move in every way possible. She understood why he was making the offer and she understood that it would not be a real marriage. And really, what did she have to lose? Homeless, penniless. Those weren't only words. They didn't express the daily fears and anxieties that grabbed her and strangled her with stress. She put on a front for Mel, who had already done so much for them, but the concept of being no longer poor shone like a brilliant, inviting sun on Lexy's horizon.

She wanted to buy her babies decent clothes, feed them the best food, put them to bed in comfortable cots. And she wanted to feel that they were safe. It crossed her mind that she would be willing to marry the devil himself to achieve those ends. Tears burned the backs of her eyes because she knew that, over the past eighteen months, she had sunk so very low in her expectations of life. If Nic was willing to sacrifice so much for his children's benefit, then it was highly probable that he would also be able to love them. And that mattered, mattered so much more than the material benefits because Lexy knew what it was like to grow up without a father's love.

'Okay,' she said stiffly. 'I'll marry you.'

CHAPTER FIVE

'GOOD HEAVENS...' Mel hissed when the cars that had met them off the helicopter drove them along a paved lane towards the giant villa studded with fancy pillars. It towered like a monolith on the heights of the hill on the island of Faros. It was Nic's home on the island, not the even larger house at the other end of it, which belonged to his elder half-brother, Jace, and their grandmother. The house Nic had inherited had only been built in the first place because their father, Argus, had fallen out with his mother, Electra.

'Prepare yourself for a very extravagant setting,' Nic had advised humorously on the phone. 'It's my house now but it's all grand Roman splendour. My father didn't do good taste.'

The two cars came to a halt. Yes, *two* cars. Nic had hired three nannies, *three*, he explained because he didn't want any nanny to feel overworked taking care of their children and he wanted every one of their babies to receive the very best care. Lexy's head was still spinning at all the changes that had taken place in her world over the past two weeks. Yes, only two weeks, not only to refill her skeletal wardrobe and buy all the bridal finery, but also to organise what had sounded like a very big wedding. Luckily her input had not been much required aside from a couple of phone calls to establish the food she liked and the colours and flowers she preferred.

'It's like being on another planet,' Mel had said at one point of Lexy's rags-to-riches transformation.

Even better, she had told herself often, Nic had achieved all the arrangements with her by phone. A much safer way to maintain their tenuous at best relationship, she reasoned, keeping it like a straightforward business arrangement, an agreement, a *deal*. His money in exchange for what he deemed to be respectability, which was marriage and fakery. He had warned her on that score too that she would have to pretend that they were keen on each other.

And how difficult could that possibly be when he looked the way he did and she was challenged to take her attention off him when he was in the same room? Nor did it take into account the number of times when, purely for reference purposes, she had looked up some of those photos of Nic online and learned stuff about him that she hadn't bothered to access when he had ghosted her eighteen months earlier. Like his name at birth had been the Italian Domenico and his mother, Bianca, had been a minor socialite in Rome when she'd first met his father. Little stuff, she consoled herself in explanation, that she had needed to know for the wedding and the people she would meet.

As the car drew up, she glimpsed an entire group of people waiting and her backbone melted like snow in summer. All those people, all those rich, important people, who had to believe that she was something she was not in Nic's eyes. She smoothed damp palms down over her designer dress, a muted shade of green teamed with wedge heels, and began to climb out as the door opened. And then she glanced up and realised that it was Nic opening the door and her sense of relief at seeing him was so intense after so many days that it left her dizzy.

'Nic…' she muttered as she stepped away from the door.

'Lexy,' he said, a literal five seconds before he swept her into his arms, whereupon he lifted her up to him to overcome their difference in height and kissed her.

And it was everything she had tried to forget, everything she had refused to relive. It was as though he lit a torch inside her and it blazed out of control. It had been so long since she had been touched that way that she dropped into that kiss with all the self-preservation of a drowning swimmer. His lips moved over hers, soft and firm and so erotic her toes curled inside her shoes and they fell off without her noticing. She grabbed his head, rediscovering the luxuriant depths of black hair she had previously sunk her hands into with pleasure. His tongue twined with hers and breathtaking heat swept up through her, a slow-burn effect pooling warmth between her thighs. Her head fell back as she gasped in oxygen.

'Get a room,' an unfamiliar voice said nearby.

Sudden awareness flooded back to Lexy and she blinked, registering belatedly that she and Nic had a sizeable audience. Embarrassment swallowed her alive. 'Put me down,' she mumbled.

'You lost your shoes,' Nic dared to remind her, and as soon as he set her down she scrabbled at his feet to relocate them.

How had he noticed the shoes when she hadn't even registered the wretched things falling off? She was mortified beyond belief. What a way to greet the in-laws! She understood, however, why Nic had gone in for the display. It was only part of the faking that he had mentioned would be part and parcel of the whole charade of marrying him. He expected them to look like a convincing couple and how else could he achieve that? Even so, had he had to fall on her like a ravenous beast the instant she appeared? Wasn't that overkill?

'Lexy, meet my brother, Jace…and his wife, Gigi.'

'Welcome to your own home,' the slender young woman told her with a big, warm smile of apology. 'I can't wait for the wedding tomorrow.'

'By the looks of it, neither can they,' Jace quipped,

and Lexy's face turned an even hotter pink. 'I was waiting for the movie cameras to start rolling.'

'Yes, it was so romantic,' the little silver-haired older lady who had joined them said brightly and Lexy found herself enfolded in a hug. 'I'm Electra, Nic's grandmother, but you can call me Yaya like my grandsons do.'

Nic led the way upstairs through a splendid marble foyer ornamented with grand and very large pieces of gilded furniture, a backdrop that would have looked more at home in a museum or a palace than on a small Greek island. Imposing and impressive it certainly was, but nothing about the ambience was comfortable or welcoming.

He paused at the door of an upstairs room and ushered her in. 'For the children,' he said with quiet satisfaction.

And there it was in front of her: the nursery of her dreams, complete with beautiful cots and all the pretty pieces of baby paraphernalia she had not been able to afford. Lexy gasped, fingering the edge of a polished wood cot, stroking a soft, smooth cotton cover. 'Was this where you grew up?' she couldn't help asking.

'No, I had this done specially for the triplets. This house wasn't built until I was an adolescent. I've already made arrangements to have three separate bedrooms prepared for Ethan, Ezra and Lily for when or if you choose to divide them.'

'My goodness, you've really been busy,' she framed unevenly, taken aback that he was already thinking ahead into their babies' futures.

'I'll show you our rooms,' Nic murmured, a hand closing over hers as the nannies began piling in with the baggage carried by a uniformed staff member.

'It's all very formal here,' she remarked.

'My father's preference, not mine. While we're here, feel free to change anything. On previous visits, I preferred to stay with Jace and Electra in the other house,' he admitted wryly. 'This was never a happy place for me.'

'Oh…' And she wanted to ask questions and know more but was that really appropriate in a fake marriage? Just at that moment, her mouth still tingling from his, and gripped by embarrassment at how she had surrendered into that kiss with more enthusiasm than strictly necessary, she decided it was better *not* to ask and to respect boundaries.

'This is you…' As her luggage was trekked in past them by more uniformed staff, Lexy gazed wide-eyed at the vast bedroom, decked out in gold, and the extreme grandeur of the gilded four-poster, and she giggled. 'Well, it's not really me,' she almost whispered. 'I feel a little ordinary looking at this.'

'My mother said she liked it, but then she was required to like it to please my father,' Nic told her. 'But she was a farm girl from a country town and I would suspect she must've felt a little overpowered as well.'

'A *farm* girl?' Lexy questioned in surprise before she could bite back the query. 'But I read that she was a socialite—'

'No, no. That was a face-saving fiction dreamt up by my father and aired because he could not have said that *he* had stooped to marry a farm girl, whom he met at a market.'

'And obviously he fell for her there,' Lexy completed.

'He was married and supposedly crazy about Jace's mother, so I suppose it depends on your viewpoint.'

'I think you're...' Lexy hesitated.

Nic studied her expectantly. 'I'm what?'

Lexy winced. 'Possibly a little too overly negative about your father, but maybe he *was* an all-round horror of a man—'

'That is how I see him. He was a man who did terrible things to a lot of people,' Nic said tightly, sinking her stomach with that admission about his parent. 'I operate very differently in business and in my own life.'

Lexy nodded, grateful to have not offended him. 'On that note, I shall be comfortable in this bedroom even if the décor is a touch overwhelming.'

'My room is through the communicating door but it's locked. I'm afraid I can't conserve your privacy tomorrow night because there is no way Yaya will put a bride and groom into separate bedrooms and as they're holding the wedding for us—'

'It's fine. We'll survive,' Lexy hastened to soothe even though her brain was exploding with confused questions.

This was the guy she had first met. Considerate, thoughtful and kind. Where had that guy gone during her barrage of phone calls, letters and office visits over eighteen months? Had Nic Diamandis simply *panicked* at the news of her pregnancy? Had he blocked her calls and dumped her letters because he couldn't face the problems her pregnancy would create? What else was she supposed to think if she was no longer able to think of him as an inherently bad, irresponsible man who thought only of himself?

Of course, he couldn't defend himself for such reprehensible behaviour, but if he was trying to make good now and make up for it, shouldn't she at least recognise the effort he was making to redress the damage he had done?

'It's a family dinner this evening hosted by Jace and my grandmother at their place.'

'What do I wear?'

'Something long and glam,' Nic advised as he departed again. 'I'll send in some jewellery for you to choose…a couple of things to use. My mother sent it here. Bang a ring on your engagement finger. It will look better.'

'Your mother knows we're fake?'

'No, my mother thinks we're real and that we ran

out of time, choosing to skip the engagement phase,'
Nic murmured ruefully. 'She's a romantic.'

*And I was as well, until I met you and then you
let me down*, Lexy reflected in suppressed anguish.

She had fallen in love in the space of an evening.
Who did that? Which sane, intelligent woman would
do that? But she had paid the price for that foolish-
ness, hadn't she? She had had many months to ago-
nise over her disillusionment.

She went back to the nursery to spend time with
her babies and get to know the nannies a little better.
Beth, Susie and Indira were young, active and chatty
and Ethan, Ezra and Lily were calm and content in
their care, which was fortunate when it was the wedding tomorrow and they would see little of her, she
reminded herself. For a while she strolled around the
house, getting acquainted with rooms, and when she
had wasted enough time, she went back to her room
to dress for dinner.

A large handsome jewellery box sat on the dresser
awaiting her. From Nic's mother, she assumed, thinking that it was a very generous woman who just offered her own possessions to a future daughter-in-law
she had yet to meet. A farm girl, fancy that. But possibly Bianca Diamandis mightn't like to be reminded
of her more humble beginnings and Nic should have
kept that info to himself.

Thinking such thoughts, Lexy picked out a kind of
blingy diamond and emerald ring and threaded it on

her ring finger to try before setting it aside to wear. Evidently, Nic had told his mother that she didn't own any jewellery. What a very kind gesture! She picked a slender diamond necklace for the neckline of the dress she planned to wear before heading for a shower and a thorough grooming.

Finding her babies already sleeping in their cots, she sighed, wishing she had made it in time for a goodnight cuddle, but she would be up very early the next morning to attend to them all. Fully gowned and feeling incredibly opulent but ill at ease in a long silvery blue dress with its mermaid skirt, which made it impossible to take anything other than very small steps, she descended the sweeping staircase to where Nic awaited her in a dinner jacket and bow tie, looking exactly as he looked in all those online photos.

Except just for once he lacked that recurring arm ornament, Angeliki Bouras, a woman who in normal circumstances Lexy would have asked a lot about. What was so special about the exquisite blonde apart from the obvious? Why did Nic's relationship with her appear to survive when other women seemed to last mere weeks in his company? Unfortunately, Lexy was aware that she had no right to ask such nosy, personal questions of a man about to make a fake marriage to her.

Nic was enthralled by the vision of Lexy in that dress with diamonds glittering at her throat and on her hand. 'You look amazing,' he said.

'I look like a gold-digger,' his future bride told him tartly. 'All got up in a designer dress sporting all this bling.'

Nic grinned, that breath-stealing grin she remembered, and her heart hammered. 'Maybe I've got a thing for sexy little gold-diggers...who knew?'

'Stop it or I'll laugh and I'm trying so hard to be refined and serene,' she admitted.

'They're only people, good and bad, friendly or unfriendly. Wealth doesn't make them one whit better than you and that's the only difference,' he said soothingly as he tucked her into a low-slung scarlet sports car and drove off.

The massive villa at the other end of the island had an elegance that his father's house did not. Nic parked outside it and handed her out. 'Show's on now. Fake it until you make it.'

'But you haven't even told me what our story's supposed to be.'

'I kept it simple. Lost your phone number, lost touch, turned the city upside down trying to find you and then, bullseye, here you are with my children,' Nic proffered lightly. 'The love of my life.'

'Do we have to exaggerate?'

'The only people here who matter are my immediate family. Jace and Gigi. My mother, Yaya. Oh, yes, and my best friend, Angeliki.'

Wow, *best* friend, well, she hadn't guessed that

likelihood very well, had she? Relieved by that news, Lexy smiled. 'I'll do my best.'

But from the first frozen glance from Angeliki's fine dark eyes, Lexy registered that the beautiful blonde might be her bridegroom's best friend, but she was never going to be equally chummy with his bride-to-be. Clad in a fabulous bronze evening gown, the Greek heiress outshone every other female present and Lexy was relieved to be warmly hugged by Nic's mother, Bianca, a diminutive brunette with a bubbly, positive personality and a bunch of chatter.

Bianca refused to be thanked for the loan of her jewellery. 'I remembered how overpowered I felt by the Diamandis tribe just after Argus married me and I couldn't have my daughter-in-law feeling the same way,' she chattered cheerfully with an openness that was utterly unexpected in such a glittering array of high-society guests. 'I'm relieved that my son saw through the façade of the often spoiled, entitled little madams he meets and married a young woman with a job and independence.'

'That's great,' Lexy said weakly as she was enthusiastically grabbed into a hug, thinking that it was not the time to mention that independence and a proper job were a long way behind her since the birth of her sons and her daughter.

'And if I promise to come really early and not interfere in anything bridal, can I please come and see my grandchildren tomorrow morning?' Bianca continued winningly. 'I'm just gasping to meet them, but I didn't want to be too pushy and wait at Nic's house today for the opportunity.'

'You're not being pushy at all,' Lexy assured her. 'You will be very welcome.

'I like your mum,' she murmured to Nic as they took their seats at the formal dining table.

'She's lovely, isn't she?' Jace's wife, Gigi, volunteered cheerfully. 'Next to Yaya, she's a favourite. Neither of them judge or criticise or bitch.'

'Electra Diamandis is a lady from head to toe. She has bred-in-the-bone class,' Angeliki interposed crushingly from across the table.

Gigi rolled speaking eyes at Lexy and she almost giggled at the blonde's snobbish intercession. The foolish woman didn't seem to grasp that it was an insult to exclude Nic's mother from such a compliment. 'And Bianca is simply pure charm and warmth,' Lexy commented.

The meal proceeded at a stately pace and Lexy noted that Angeliki rarely removed her attention from Nic, regularly addressing little witty comments in excluding Greek to him while studiously ignoring Lexy's existence. No, definitely not friendship material.

It was a longish evening. There was a lot of meeting and greeting after the food was eaten. Lexy was flagging by the time Nic intimated that it was time to leave and she had gone out to the hall to retrieve her evening wrap when Angeliki approached her. 'It won't last—you and Nic,' she spelt out thinly.

'And I want your opinion because...?' Lexy countered.

'He only wants those children. I'm warning you that you'll lose them if you go ahead tomorrow,' Angeliki announced with the sweetness of a viper.

Lexy merely nodded and turned away to unfurl her evening wrap and cloak her bare shoulders. But her tummy had turned over at that warning and she told herself off for being affected by a woman who very obviously wanted Nic for herself. So much for this particular female best friend, a relationship that could only work if there was a lack of attraction on both sides.

'You seem troubled,' Nic commented as he tucked her back into the car after a long trail of goodbyes.

'Not at all,' Lexy said stoically, resolved not to run telling tales, which would likely be poorly received. Unlike Angeliki, Lexy could read people, and Angeliki might want Nic but she could see that Nic did not want her back, in spite of her beauty and her lithe, shapely sexiness. 'It's just been a long day and I'm very tired.'

The next morning was Lexy's wedding day and she was still tired because she had lain awake a long time worrying that there was truth in Angeliki's nasty suggestion. How far could she trust Nic in believing that he would not try to remove her children from her care in their eventual divorce? And in truth, that was not yet an answer she could give. Yet, bearing in mind her financial struggles over the past eighteen months, she did not believe she had a choice because it was her duty, just as much as it was *his*, to ensure that their children had a more stable, secure home. But she could not credit that Nic would want to risk hurting his children by depriving them in any way of their mother.

She found Bianca Diamandis down on her knees in the nursery playing with the triplets and sensibly clad for the occasion, so she wasn't too bothered about wearing a dressing robe herself. Sitting down on the rug with Bianca, she helped Ethan, Ezra and Lily get to know their grandmother. As she returned to her room, she met Nic in the corridor, tall and darkly handsome in a cotton sweater and tight jeans.

He held a finger to his wide firm lips in a silencing gesture. 'Bride and groom aren't supposed to see each other before the church,' he told her.

Lexy flushed and disappeared into her bedroom again, deciding that so far she wasn't doing very well in the 'faking it' stakes because until now the concept of such traditions had passed her by. Mel awaited her, having ducked out of the dinner the night before because she had said she wouldn't be comfortable in such lofty company. But Lexy was tempted to tell her that she had felt perfectly comfortable, with the single exception of Angeliki's shrewish approach.

Her beautiful gown hung awaiting her but a small procession of professionals was due first to do her hair, her make-up and her nails.

'So, how do you feel about this now?' Mel prompted, for her best friend was not entirely sure she should trust Nic enough to believe that he would only do right by her and his children.

'Moderately hopeful,' Lexy confided. 'He's making an effort and I can see it. It may be happening a bit late in the day, but you can only applaud a guy brave enough to say that he's quite happy for me to marry him for his money.'

'Either that or he's a very devious character,' Mel remarked, predictably less tolerant as a lawyer, having stood by Lexy during her worst experiences during the crucial eighteen months of Nic's absence.

The bridal preparation team arrived then and there was no time for further personal conversation. Within a couple of hours, Lexy was viewing herself with Bianca's diamond tiara anchoring the short veil she wore to the back of her head, letting her dress, which she loved, do its thing without further embellishment. She had reasoned that it might well be her only wedding gown ever and, with cost no object, she had shopped for her fantasy. Fashioned of sequinned silk tulle and delicate embroidery, it had the slender silhouette of an Edwardian tea dress with a fitted boat-shaped bodice and long tight sleeves, shaping her figure without burying her in loads of fabric that would only accentuate her lack of height.

'You look stupendous,' Mel told her dreamily.

As Lexy paused at the foot of the aisle in the large village church, she viewed the packed pews and lifted her head high. One of Jace's uncles had offered to fill in for her absent father, whom she had not bothered to invite, but Lexy had politely declined the offer because she was giving herself away, not depending on some male figure to take charge of her.

But as Nic turned his proud dark head to look at her, she felt a reaction she knew she shouldn't feel to the seemingly stunned appraisal he was dealing her. Gosh, he was good at faking it, she thought in admiration. Really, *really* good…

CHAPTER SIX

THE WEDDING CEREMONY was formal and relatively brief.

'You look very beautiful,' Nic murmured in the sunlight on the steps afterwards while the photographer snapped pictures.

'You don't need to fake it in private,' she assured him out of the corner of her smiling lips.

'You can't accept a compliment like any other woman?'

'Not when I'm wracked with nerves, no,' she conceded in apologetic afterthought.

He steered her through the crush into the beribboned car that would take them back to the house and the reception. 'I don't say stuff I don't mean, not even to fake it,' Nic censured.

Lexy breathed in deep and slow and scrutinised the platinum wedding ring on her finger because she *still* felt as though she were figuring in a daydream and that she couldn't possibly be legally wed to the tall, absolutely gorgeous and very wealthy man beside her.

'Nothing feels real to me today,' she said truthfully.

'I've lived a very quiet life and all this the hype, the fuss, the glitz—it's totally alien to me.'

'I only want you to feel comfortable. I can promise you that after today, there will be no hype, no fuss.'

Calming down then, she allowed him to guide her into the house where they had dined the night before, where they greeted guests as they arrived before entering a room the size of a ballroom where the meal was being staged. Caterers were everywhere.

'Did you invite your father?' Nic enquired over the first course of their meal.

Lexy froze. 'No. I contacted him shortly after I had the triplets and he wasn't interested. In fact, he gave me a lecture about irresponsibility and even though Ezra was still in the special care baby unit, he didn't want to visit him or even meet his first grandchildren. So, no, I didn't want to invite him...even though he would probably be very impressed by you because you have status and wealth,' she completed uncomfortably.

Lean, strong features taut, Nic nodded. 'I agree with your decision.'

Relieved by that response, she relaxed more. 'I've only got Mel here as a guest and I asked her parents if they wanted to come, but her father doesn't have any leave left. Really, over the past couple of years, there's been nobody else close enough to warrant a wedding invitation.'

Nic breathed in deep, carefully choosing his words,

although there was a storm brewing inside him that he was holding back. 'You've had a tough time without backup.'

The silence simmered and screamed between them and neither of them attempted to break it with adverse comments. Lexy wanted to ask him what had possessed him when he'd chosen to ignore and deny her situation. Nic wanted to ask her why she hadn't given him a chance to help her and, even worse, had chosen to lie about having given him that chance when he knew for a fact that she had not.

The wedding speeches were short and soon over. The cake was cut and served and the dancing began. They spent ages socialising before Nic closed his hand over hers and whirled her onto the floor to dance. Initially Lexy was as stiff as a tree trunk in his arms, but he eased her closer until the warmth and strength of him bled through the layers of their clothing and melted the cold knot of indecision inside her. Heat pooled at the heart of her as he moved against her, powerful thighs and narrow hips flexing. Her nipples prickled and tightened and she swallowed hard as her body went off on a wonderland of rediscovery about Nic's body without any prompting from her. In embarrassment, she tried to suppress her natural reaction to his proximity.

'Relax,' he urged huskily as she tensed again. 'This performance is almost over.'

Yes, it *was* a performance, she reminded herself

grimly, not a real wedding day and she shouldn't be responding to Nic as if he were a genuine husband or as if they were a couple in love.

Angeliki Bouras slid with a subtle sidewise movement between them. 'I need a word with you in private,' she informed Nic without embarrassment, as if it weren't the slightest bit strange to part the bride and groom on the dance floor.

Irritation assailed Nic. Sometimes, Angeliki had the worst sense of timing, he thought as she urged him out of the ballroom and into Jace's library across the hall.

'What is it?' Nic asked with an impatience he tried to mask out of politeness.

Angeliki smiled wide and bright, tossing her long blonde tresses back over one slim shoulder, dark eyes intent. 'I felt it was time to give you some advice… now that you're married without having *wanted* to get married.'

That latter statement was truer than he wished and Angeliki actually voicing the fact set his teeth on edge. 'I don't need advice.'

'Obviously you got married to secure your children. Three of them—*Theos mou*, couldn't she have been less productive?' Angeliki mocked with a wince of distaste as though fertility were a vulgar topic. 'So what now? If you're wondering, I can help.'

'I'm not in need of any help,' Nic cut in firmly.

'If you live with your bride, you'll be *stuck* with her,' Angeliki pointed out. 'That's not what you want.'

'You don't know what I want,' Nic sliced in with finality, already swinging round to return to the door and leave her.

'I'm thinking of what will make you happy,' Angeliki declared, impressively enough that he turned his head back, warm dark eyes seeking his with sympathy. 'I advise you to stash your unwanted bride in one of your many houses—say that lovely chateau in France—and leave her there to be Mrs Diamandis on her own. And then you continue with your life just as you like it, your freedom reclaimed.'

Nic frowned, exasperated by her interfering advice. 'My plans with my wife and children are none of your business, Angeliki. However, your outlook is ridiculously limited. For a start, I have three children who will *always* be my children and I must act as their father. That's my role in life. My father didn't do it for me, but I will not be found lacking in the parental role when it comes to my children,' he asserted grimly, ignoring her angry glower of dissatisfaction. 'Excuse me… I should be with my bride.'

Nic appeared beside Lexy again and drew her straight back onto the dance floor. 'Sorry about that. Angeliki was being a drama queen.'

'Does she make a habit of that?'

'More often than I find comfortable. I can still recall her screaming tantrums when we were kids,' he confided with a chuckle. 'She prefers to be the centre of attention.'

'And she's not likely to get that at our wedding,' Lexy remarked, wishing he weren't quite so fond of the beautiful blonde, who could only treat his bride like wallpaper.

Nic drew her close and the ripples of heat filtered through her, relaxing her body again. No matter how hard she tried to stifle her response, it deepened in strength. She stole a glance up at him and his dark eyes were a stunning blaze of gold between dense black lashes and her mouth ran dry, her breath shortening in her tight throat.

With a muttered phrase that could have been an imprecation in his own language, Nic lowered his head. 'When you look at me like this...'

With scant warning, his mouth crushed hers and she quivered in the shelter of his arms, instinctively pressing closer, shaken to appreciate that he appeared to be as aroused as she was. The press of his long thickness against her abdomen sent a faint shiver rippling through her because it had been so long since she had been touched, so long since that night when she had discovered that she was a much more sexual being than she had ever dreamt. Recollections lingered no matter how hard she tried to shut them down and forget them.

Nic steered her off the floor into the shelter of one of pillars that edged the big room, providing quieter seating areas and shadowy spaces. He spread her back against the pillar and kissed her with a depth of hunger that she was utterly unprepared to meet. Desire melted her like a hot pool of honey spreading in her pelvis.

Nic lifted his head, black hair messily tousled by her roaming fingers. 'I want you,' he admitted thickly.

The tension and insecurity she had fought off all day took fire from that blunt admission. It felt really good that he wanted her to such an extent. At that moment, it seemed as though it validated her, made their marriage truly human and more real. The connection that had linked them the night that she had conceived their children was still there in spades and she couldn't fight it off.

'Escape is only twenty feet away,' a familiar voice murmured without any expression at all.

'I beg your pardon?' Lexy almost whispered as she jerked her mouth free of Nic's addictive taste.

From a couple of feet away, his brother, Jace, dealt her a wide smile. 'You two can leave. You've ticked every box. The bride and groom are free to slip away now.'

Her face now hot as hellfire, Lexy swallowed hard.

'*Seriously*, Jace?' Nic quipped.

'Rear staircase behind that door at the foot,' Jace informed his brother. 'Thought you might not be aware of that exit as you didn't spend much time here as a boy.'

Nic said something in Greek and grinned wick-edly down at her. He bent down and, before she could even guess what he intended to do, he scooped her up into his arms.

'So discreet,' Jace teased with sincere amusement.

'He doesn't know we're fake,' Lexy muttered help-lessly as Jace strode down the room like a man on a mission.

'Doesn't need to know. He only knows that we've had enough of the festivities. And possibly that we can't keep our hands off each other.'

Speak for yourself, she almost said in disagree-ment, but he set her down on her feet again on a small landing up a narrow staircase, and while she was striving to muster a sensible thought with which to prop up her sinking dignity, Nic dragged her back into his arms for another hungry, driving kiss that splintered through her trembling length like a bolt of lightning, burning and racing through every nerve ending in her body. His long fingers, his big strong hands ranged over her curves as he bent down to her, and her heart was hammering so hard she was scared that it might pound right out of her chest.

'Do you want me?' he breathed raggedly.

And there it was: the opportunity to call a halt. But Lexy was no hypocrite, no liar. 'I want you,' she muttered unsteadily, wondering how she could still be that vulnerable, questioning whether a retreat into cold dignity would somehow magically persuade her otherwise. Unfortunately for her, a stronger urge was warring for dominance inside her. It was a crazy *what the hell?* feeling, absolutely new to her sane and sensible self.

Unmistakeable satisfaction slashed Nic's wide sensual mouth and his dark golden eyes glimmered bright with admiration. 'You didn't lie, play games—'

'I *don't*,' she cut in as he urged her up the stairs.

As she paused at the top of the steps to catch her breath, he captured her parted lips afresh and her temperature rocketed, desire coiled up tight within her, urging her to reach up and frame his lean, dark face with her hands. He lifted her off her feet and into his arms again, striding down a wide, imposing hallway full of paintings. 'Yaya's art gallery,' he proffered with humorous brevity as he thrust wide a door into a bedroom.

It contained a massive bed decked out in pristine white sheets. Rice and almonds and flower buds were scattered across it.

'Rice and almonds for happiness and prosperity,' Nic informed her as he shook the sheet clear of the offerings. 'Yaya likes the ancient traditions.'

'Well, you don't really need to be hoping for the prosperity,' Lexy pointed out.

Nic flung back his darkly handsome head and laughed outright at that truth. Heavens, he was breathtaking in that moment, so gorgeous, she couldn't credit that he was now her husband. But her husband for how long? Lexy squashed that thought, all of a quiver with conflicting emotions and feelings, her body taut. There was a little voice in the back of her head warning her that, married or otherwise, she should not be even considering sharing a bed again with the father of her children. Lifting her chin, she glanced across the room at him, and common sense wasn't worth anything when he was *still* her fantasy, she conceded ruefully.

There had been little to celebrate beyond the health and happiness of her children in the months since they had last been together. All that time she had felt as though she were simply running to keep up and by the end of it, after infinite months empty of the smallest adult fun, she had felt as old as the hills. And there Nic Diamandis stood, jerking loose his bow tie, toeing off his shoes, with the kind of confident insouciance that should have set her on fire with rage and resentment...only it didn't. Everything about Nic Diamandis set her on fire sexually. That calm, innate assurance, that cool, sophisticated edge, that deep-pitched sonorous drawl of his, the devastating good looks, not even to mention the unexpected kindness and understanding he could give. She told herself that she was doing something for *her*, not for him, not for the children, something just purely for her.

After all, why would she care about how he felt? This guy who had used her to provide him with entertainment on a snowy, forgotten night in Yorkshire?

That was all 'they' had been, no matter how hard she had tried to believe otherwise in the disillusioning months that had followed. She could use him as well to fill the emptiness inside her chest, the loneliness that sometimes bit very deep. He didn't need to know that *she* needed more, *cared* more than that. And in addition, she was far from stupid, well aware that an unconsummated marriage could be legally deemed to be no marriage at all when it came to severing those ties. Lawyers for rich people were paid to be very clever and only a foolish woman would ignore that reality with a divorce on the horizon.

'You're a thousand miles away...' Nic's reflection appeared behind her in the cheval mirror she had moved towards and he looked like a tall, strong, shirt-clad monolith in the dimness of the shaded windows. Tall enough to touch the sky, she would've thought as a child. But she was no longer a child and the sheer size and breadth, the inherent strength of him sent a sensual shiver through her taut frame. 'Do you need help to get out of the dress?'

'What do you think?' Lexy almost whispered, her mouth drying up again as he glanced back at the complex lacing and hook arrangements that had fitted her into her fantasy gown. She didn't know whether it was a curse or a blessing that it had not crossed her mind once that her bridegroom would have to help her get out of her dress again. It was that platonic arrangement they had agreed and where was that now?

Nic laughed again. 'I think you'd have to be a contortionist to get out of it alone.'

The first few hooks began to loosen the fit of the gown. He might have big hands, but he had precise fingers, she recognised as the lacing tightness round her ribcage eased, fingertips swiped smoothly across her shoulders, and without warning the whole dress was dropping, pooling round her feet like a statement, leaving her clad in the tasteful bits of nothing much that were all the dress design had allowed.

'A garter.'

Nic knelt down behind her, making her ludicrously aware of her wispy lace strapless bra and knickers and the pull-up pale stockings, over one of which was layered a 'something blue garter', a gift from Mel, even though her friend was aware that she was not a real bride. Mel, as Lexy had become, was a cynic and had agreed that this might be Lexy's only ever wedding.

'I didn't think you'd even be wearing one.'

'You don't know that much about me,' Lexy said, enjoying that truth, enjoying that he didn't know how much tougher she had got, how much she had changed from that gentle, forgiving person she had once been.

'I'm willing to learn,' Nic husked, trailing the garter down to a dainty ankle, freeing her foot from her shoe to thread it off, pausing only to gently extract her other foot from its shoe. Had she been the kind of woman who still believed in her fairy-tale prince she would have been swooning, weak at the knees from his aplomb and smooth words. Only now she wasn't that naïve.

He vaulted upright again, snapped loose her bra and it fell away. His hands rose to cup her breasts, her nipples straining in the cooler air...and from his touch. She realised that as she had stood there thinking ever more bitter thoughts, on one level she had been trying to talk herself out of getting intimate with him again. He filled her with indecision and she was not an indecisive woman. Yet still her body hummed and throbbed that close to him, pulsing with a hunger she could not suppress, and that *was* a humbling acknowledgement.

Slowly, *very* slowly, as though he knew what was inside her head, Nic turned her round and claimed her parted lips again, swallowing what she might have said, utterly silencing whatever indecisive thoughts she might still have been feeling in his radius. When he kissed her, when he held her close, there was only him and the wild, insane attraction of him, and he drew her down on the bed with gentle hands. In that instant she was lost because he didn't push, he didn't demand, he was everything that she remembered... the guy who *cared* about how she felt.

The span of his hands over her breasts, which were fuller and rather less pert than they had once been, turned her inside out with anticipation. She was all woman, all in the control of desire in an instant, wanting, needing what he could offer. Her nipples tingled and prickled, hunger like a dam burst threatening to break penned up within her, so that her spine arched to deepen that pressure and a faint moan escaped her.

'I've never wanted any woman the way I've wanted you,' Nic husked.

And she didn't believe him, didn't care because she wanted him more than her next meal, which in times gone by, when she had gone hungry for her children, meant more than he could ever have appreciated in his gilded world of privilege and excess. He was laying her down on the bed and she almost felt like telling him that subtlety of the type he was offering was unnecessary because she was definitely a sure thing. He was the guy that had taught her, that very first night they had been together, that even when she was sore and exhausted, she could still want him with the fire of a thousand suns. And he hadn't been careful and, fool that she had been in her innocence of what a disaster an unplanned pregnancy could be, she had acquiesced. In reality, Nic Diamandis was only reaping the seeds he had sown.

'I want you too,' she admitted without the smallest embarrassment, watching him peel off his shirt, revealing a chest that belonged in a sculpture gallery, lean, honed abs and tight, taut musculature of the type rarely seen in ordinary men. No, there was nothing ordinary about Nic Diamandis, he was absolutely the dream and the fantasy she remembered, and no longer did she marvel that she had succumbed to all that pure, bronzed temptation. So what if she was looking at him as a sex object? Hadn't that only been how he must have viewed her that long ago night?

'I wasn't expecting you to be so...open,' he muttered unevenly.

'I'm not the same woman you met eighteen months ago,' she warned him.

'I see that,' he conceded, an uneasiness to the admission that pulled at her, making her wonder what he was thinking until she reminded herself that she really shouldn't care at all what he was thinking. After all, he was her husband now and where his thoughts or his heart went now was no business of hers because she wasn't looking for him to love her or essentially *care* for her. She was expecting him only to help care for their children and ensure a secure future for her and the kids. All that romantic stuff? She was done with that. The romance stuff had burned her down to the bone because she had fallen in love with a guy who truly didn't exist, not a guy who would have shied away from her and turned his back when she'd turned up inconveniently pregnant and desperate.

He unbelted his narrow-cut trousers and she rejoiced in his masculine beauty like a groupie, ashamed of herself and yet still wanting him so much. Bitterness and resentment didn't provide the barrier she had expected, she conceded ruefully, heat pulsing at the heart of her, because surely no woman had ever reasonably wanted a man as much as she still wanted him? The trousers dropped, so did the boxers and she was enthralled, because these views were what she had not seen that first time in the shadows and the darkness of the bedroom.

'I love the way you look at me,' Nic confided hoarsely, his glittering golden eyes holding her fast. 'Like you want me as much as I want you.'

'I *do*,' she confided without self-consciousness, because that wasn't a weakness, not the way she had learned to consider it. She was merely separating wanting from love and that was easy after the battles she had lived through.

'It bridges our separation,' he breathed, coming down to her, all husky, muscular, supremely aroused male, and she was mesmerised by him, no longer marvelling at the manner in which she had succumbed to him before. He was something else in terms of looks and charisma, the perfect ten if such a list of male attributes existed.

He claimed her mouth with erotic expertise, parting her lips, skating along them, only finally delving deep, and she fell into that kiss as if there were nothing beneath her, only a swirling, ever heightening world of pure sensuality. Yes, he was unbelievable in bed, she told herself, lying prone on the bed as he dallied over the swollen buds of her breasts, kissing a line down from that area to the next. Playboys didn't get to be what they were without lots of practice, she reasoned absently, struggling now to stay in touch with her brain.

'I dreamt of doing this again. Your body, it's so perfect,' he groaned.

'It's not perfect any more,' she heard herself say, wondering if he hadn't picked up on the stretchmarks on her abdomen and her breasts and even her thighs, because her body had behaved badly when she'd been pregnant with the triplets. There wasn't a part of her that hadn't swollen up way beyond perfection.

'But it's *you*,' he emphasised, as though she were still the hottest female on earth that had ever been seen.

'And it's you,' she whispered, small hands lifting to frame his high cheekbones, fingertips drifting off into the lushness of his black hair. Heavens, he was gorgeous.

Skilled fingers traced the heart of her then, probing, exploring, and he followed with the heat and expertise of his mouth. Within seconds she was lost in what he was doing to her, lost in sensation and need. Hunger burned in her pelvis like a flaming torch and she was arching and gasping and moaning and racing into climax without any input of her own.

'I want you to enjoy this,' Nic husked thickly. 'I want you to be like this with me...*always*.'

Chance would be a fine thing, she thought, struggling to get her brain back because, really, he was *that* good in bed. Not that she had anyone to compare him with but, even so, honour where it was due. She was sure there were plenty of men who left women wanting and unsatisfied, because she had listened to Mel, a veteran of several failed relationships, and she knew that the brand of sexual joy she was receiving was not universal. She knew exactly why she was putty in his expert hands: Nic knew what he was doing in bed with a woman.

He slid over her and even her sated body reacted to that provocative move, the buds on her breasts tightening again, the burn at her core reawakening, because she already knew that he could deliver... Oh, boy, could he deliver.

He lifted her legs over his shoulders and a kind of blissful anticipation enfolded her, damp heat turning her inner spaces to liquid welcome. Her heart picked up pace, the blood in her veins racing in concert, and he entered her, and there was a slight burn and a stretch. Even so, he felt amazing. Her body gave way to his as though such an intrusion was welcomed and it *was*, it was everything she had recalled in the dark of the night in private, because nobody policed her dreams.

And the substance of her dreams only got better as he moved, withdrawing and then entering again, pushing hard to the very centre of her being. Delight encased her body, a slow roll of delight she couldn't resist, no matter how hard she tried. Her hands closed over his shoulders, fingers digging in. When the next thrust came, she was so into it, she moaned, and he looked down at her with those glittering golden eyes and she was lost in the sensation, her hips shifting as though to accommodate him although he was managing fine without her input. He was going slow and she wanted more.

'Speed up,' she urged without thinking about it.

And he did and it was as amazing as everything else he had ever done with her. Mind-blowing pleasure engulfed her as her level of excitement built and built. With every fibre her body was surging to a peak, and he took her there with effortless perfection. She cried out at the height of a heart-stopping climax and he followed her with a raw male groan of completion.

'You are so unbelievably sexy,' he told her.

'It's you…as long as I don't look for anything more,' she mumbled, her body limp and sated in that aftermath of satisfaction, every defence down.

A moment after relieving Lexy of his weight, Nic slowly levered himself up and gazed down at her with scorching dark golden eyes. 'And what does that mean…exactly?' he prompted dangerously.

'Well, you already *know* what it means,' Lexy contributed, struggling to get her brain working again in the wake of that gigantic physical rush of pleasure. 'You're useless at the long haul. You're more about the short, non-committal stuff.'

The gold in his dark eyes flared to a brilliant blaze.

'That's not really what you think about me,' he assured her, seemingly impregnable in his ego.

Lexy leapt out of the bed, driven by pride and nothing else, for she could not abide allowing him to believe that, because he didn't deserve it after what he had done to her: he had deserted her when she'd needed him most. She yanked the sheet off the bed with an almighty tug and wrapped it round her because she refused to stand there naked and seemingly vulnerable—she refused to be vulnerable around Nic Diamandis again.

She lifted her chin, eyes the colour of tropical seas striking back at him in challenge. 'It *is*,' she confirmed with near pleasure, because in the moment after all that physical stuff she felt happy to be fighting him again. Indeed it felt good and made her feel better. 'You let me down when I most needed your help. I had nobody but Mel and, eventually, her parents. But I was alone, struggling through a very difficult pregnancy and unable to work from quite early on. I needed support and you weren't there for me in *any* way!'

'You didn't contact me,' Nic informed her afresh, every syllable one of biting clarity. 'You didn't give me the chance! I was not aware that you had ever tried to contact me.'

Lexy's teeth gritted. 'That argument doesn't wash,' she told him frankly. 'I phoned your office. I even tried to make appointments with you there and the closest I got to seeing you was getting out of the lift on the top floor before I was discreetly removed by your security guards and taken back downstairs and shown back onto the street. I was very pregnant at the time. It wasn't the warmest welcome to your workplace.'

'My security staff would *not* manhandle a pregnant woman,' Nic declared with the utmost confidence.

'Oh, there was no manhandling involved,' Lexy agreed. 'The guards were respectful and polite and, I suspect, very embarrassed, but it was made quite clear to me that I must not return to the premises. And I *didn't*. That was the day I gave up on you showing some spine.'

'I beg your pardon?' At that offensive charge, Nic vaulted out of bed in a colossal surge of temper, dark golden eyes now burning like flames, lean, dark features rigid with incredulity.

'You heard me,' Lexy said, her mouth running dry but that didn't silence her. 'I'm finally being honest with you about how I feel. I was six months pregnant and the size of a house. I was supposed to be on bedrest, but I gave it up that day to make one last attempt to reach you, and you know how that turned out, so please stop trying to pretend that the guy who rejected me and ignored me was a nice guy...because you're *not*.'

Nic was studying her with fixed intensity. 'I cannot believe I'm even listening to this nonsense.'

'Right,' Lexy murmured, noticeably unimpressed

by that rejoinder. 'You want me to put all that in the past and bury it because now you've changed your mind, but life doesn't work like that, Nic. People don't work like that either. You blocked my phone calls, and you ignored my letters and my requests to see you at work—because I didn't know where you lived in London. You *ghosted* me, and, no matter how reasonable or kind you are now, it'll take a long time for me to forget being treated like I was a nobody, a nuisance and a burden you *couldn't* accept!'

Nic breathed in so deep in a visible effort to maintain self-control that she was frozen to the spot watching that struggle. Beneath her stressed-out gaze, he retrieved his boxers and his dress trousers, pulling them on in quick economic movements, lean bronzed muscles flexing as he dressed and reached for his shirt. 'That's not what happened and you know it,' he told her flatly. 'You didn't try to contact me. If you'd come to my office even once, I would have been told about it.'

Silenced by that protest but unimpressed, Lexy shrugged a dismissive shoulder.

Nic's mouth compressed. 'I'll use another room tonight,' he spelt out in a raw undertone, fighting the incendiary urge to call her a liar again. 'I refuse to exchange words with you when you're in this mood.'

'It's not a mood. It's an actual sense of bitterness and you made me like this,' Lexy declared, wincing when her voice almost hit a note of apology because no way was she taking back anything that she had claimed. 'But perhaps it's best you sleep somewhere else... Won't someone notice that the bridal couple are sleeping apart?'

'What do you care?' Nic fired back at her, bristling like a panther someone had had the nerve to try and stroke like a pet.

Lexy's complexion switched from flushed to very pale and she straightened her already stiff spine even more. 'I'm sorry I haven't been better at pretending to be a real bride,' she muttered truthfully. 'But I have feelings like everyone else and right now I'd prefer to be with my children.'

'*My* children as well!' Nic exhaled audibly, surveying her with hard, dark eyes and a tight mouth, his jawline tight as a bowstring and as hard as a rock. 'In half an hour a car will collect you at the rear exit. I will send a maid up to escort you there and you can make a discreet return to our children for what remains of the night. But be warned, we all have a *very* early start in the morning. We're flying to South Korea for a week. I have business there.'

Thrown into disbelief by that sudden string of disclosures, Lexy merely watched as he departed. *South Korea?* Her birthplace and her home for years? What was that about?

Nic hadn't said one word that she'd expected him to say, which both infuriated and frustrated her because she wanted him to frankly admit why he had behaved as he had during her pregnancy. But possibly she was being naïve again. They might have just set the bed on fire together but theirs was not a real relationship. It was a marriage of convenience, not a marriage of true love. Why would he strip himself bare of his pride and admit that he had made mistakes and ignored her when she'd needed him?

Yet only honesty could bridge the gulf of bitter resentment between them. She knew he wasn't a superhero, and she wasn't hoping for him to turn into one either but, at the very least, she deserved better than what he had so far given her, she told herself heavily.

She began to look for clothing to put on beyond her discarded bridal regalia. With a grimace, she made use of one of the robes hanging in the sumptuous bathroom. It would do fine for sneaking out some rear exit late at night, she told herself ruefully.

CHAPTER SEVEN

LEXY WAS HALF asleep when she boarded the private jet for the very long flight to South Korea. The nannies were like walking zombies and the triplets were all asleep.

Lexy had spent what remained of her wedding night in the gilded four-poster alone and wide awake and she blamed Nic for that unfortunate fact. Nic Diamandis, her *husband*, strange as that truth still was to accept, was, even now, set on concrete denial of his past misdeeds. How could she possibly work with that? In reality, there was no way. But at the same time, Lexy was awash with self-loathing and impatience over the part she had played. The last thing she should have done with her fake husband was stage a giant confrontation on their wedding night. That had definitely been a badly timed and poorly executed move.

What had possessed her?

Unhappily, Lexy was well aware of why she had lost control of her tongue. Nic had dared to behave as though everything were normal between them when it was anything but! She had been spread paper thin in the moments after she had retrieved her wits following their renewed intimacy. All right, she had been upset, torn apart by the awareness that she had succumbed yet again to Nic's sexual charisma. A woman abandoned to give birth alone to triplets the first time could not have an excuse for voluntarily signing up for more of the same casual sex. What else could it be with a guy like that? Nor did the fact that they were now legally married somehow justify her self-destructive behaviour.

There she had been making all those excuses to herself when, quite clearly, she had merely fallen yet again for Nic's irresistible quality. How could she still find him irresistible? That alone was unforgivable. Where was her pride? Her dignity?

Lexy shot a narrow-eyed glance across the aisle to where Nic sat working at his laptop. They had all had breakfast as a party, with the conference room onboard his private jet serving as a dining room. Casually dressed in designer jeans and shirt, Nic had got down on the floor there to play with his sons and daughter afterwards and, later, had even borrowed Lily from a nanny to help feed them. Yes, he was definitely aiming at the Daddy of the Year award, Lexy conceded. Even though she felt mean having that thought she was unable to stifle it after the manner in which they had parted the night before.

After all, aside from polite and unavoidable acknowledgements, the new bride was now being ignored. Perhaps he liked to remind her that she was only a bride in other people's eyes. Just as when she got the chance she would remind Nic that the only reason she had slept with him was to ensure that their marital ties were fully legal in terms of a later divorce. That was the sole way that she could save face, she told herself angrily. If he couldn't admit the truth of his own faults to her, why should *she* be honest?

Why would she admit that when she took even a glance at his strong, perfect profile or his shimmering dark eyes it virtually stopped her brain in its tracks? Or that she was a particular fan of his physique clad in form-fitting jeans that enhanced and outlined every lean, muscular line of his compelling masculinity? Or that she didn't have to think very long to recall the hard, erotic surge of him inside her the night before and that even the memory of that intimacy made her feel hot and damp all over and sex-obsessed? Those were matters that she had to keep private for the sake of her own sanity.

A fleet of limousines met them off the runway and they all piled in to speed down the motorway to Seoul. 'Aside from business, why did you choose to bring us here?' she heard herself ask, because she just could not contain her curiosity.

'Originally this was intended as a pleasure trip. It's your birthplace and the culture in which you grew up. I believed you would enjoy rediscovering it.'

'That was a very kind thought,' Lexy said stiltedly and kicked herself for asking because, really, he was always determined to portray himself as a nice, decent guy even if he wasn't.

'And then a tech company in which I'm particularly interested came up as a possibility and the business angle took over.' Nic shot her a glance from level dark golden eyes. 'You see, I didn't have to be truthful about that, but please note that I *was*. I'm not a liar, Lexy. I never have been and I never will be because my father lied at the drop of a hat to my mother, to me, to friends and employees and I have a strong distaste for those who choose to go through life fooling and deceiving others.'

The atmosphere was so tense as he made that little speech that Lexy tried and failed to swallow. His level, hard gaze burned into hers and she looked away hurriedly. Colour washed up over her face because what could she possibly say in response to *that*?

From the first night they'd met and he'd pretended that she meant more to him than she actually did, Nic Diamandis had been lying to her in one way or another. According to him, he had never received her letters or her calls, nor had he blocked her visits. And possibly he was *never* planning to tell the truth on that score, she reflected with a sinking stomach. He was a billionaire, highly successful in every field. Why would he strip himself bare of his pride and arrogance for her sake? Why on earth would he ever admit that he had panicked like a teenager at the prospect of a sickly pregnant woman he had never expected to hear from again? And a woman carrying children he had not planned to have?

It was equally possible that he hadn't panicked, she conceded. Perhaps there had been some other secret reason why he'd been determined to keep her out of his life and if that were true, would she ever be told? Her triangular face tightening, she sat very still and continued to say nothing.

Nic compressed his wide sensual mouth and said smoothly, 'So, have you got friends to look up while you're here?'

He was holding onto his temper by a hair's breadth, weary of her refusal to concede that she had not made any attempt to contact him after that night in York-shire. He reminded himself that he had lost the means to contact *her* and that it was highly likely that she had made the worst possible deductions from his silence. But why the hell, if she was suffering through what sounded like a very difficult pregnancy, wouldn't she have still approached him for help? For the first time it occurred to him that that just didn't compute be-cause, right from the start, Lexy had impressed him as a rather practical young woman with sound com-mon sense.

'It's a bit late for that. I left Seoul when I was fif-teen,' she reminded him wryly. 'I didn't have a best friend here. My father wouldn't let me even go out shopping with other girls and my mother only accepted visitors at home when Dad needed her to host his business dinners. It was quite a restricted upbringing, off to school and then back home to do my homework and study. I wasn't very good at maths, so there was a *lot* of studying and tutors and extra classes and all the rest of it. The school day is long in Seoul.'

Lexy was not exaggerating. Her father had taken the smallest sign of her failing to excel in any subject to heart and she still broke out in a cold sweat remembering him telling her over and over again what a stupid girl she was when it came to algebra. His expectations of her had never been met, no matter how hard she'd worked.

'To be fair though,' she added, because she hated to sound weak, 'top academic results are very much a thing here with parents, and children are expected to study hard.'

'I will need you to work as an interpreter here for me,' Nic admitted grudgingly because, really, at that moment, he didn't wish to be beholden to her for any assistance, but at least they were talking again, which was preferable to the reverse. He had no desire to live with Lexy in a state of sustained hostility. That would scarcely aid his resolve to act as a proper father to his children. And that was where his relationship with Lexy would begin and end, he promised himself fiercely. The wedding-night passion had been a crucial error, a case of both of them messing up what should have remained a platonic marriage.

It was dark and the night sky was already lighting up with the approach to Seoul, a city that rejoiced in a great number of skyscrapers because it was ringed in mountains and land was at a premium. The limo sped along city streets. There were neon-lit advertisements and bright lights everywhere and occasional glimpses into packed shopping streets. But most of all, Lexy felt the busy buzz and hum of an Asian city that literally never slept.

'Where are we staying?' she asked abruptly as she recognised the exclusive streets of Gangnam. It was the wealthiest district in Seoul.

'I hired a house large enough to cope with the size of entourage we require travelling,' Nic told her with an amused quirk to his sculpted mouth. 'And live-in staff to keep the household running. Not a hotel, but it should be close enough to offer you some pampering.'

Lexy stiffened. 'I don't need pampering.'

'You've been living hand to mouth for a long time. Of course you do. I appreciate that you put our children first in everything but that does not leave me ignorant of what you must've gone without.'

'How on earth do you even know that?' Lexy shot at him furiously and then comprehension sank in as she recalled seeing him chatting to her friend at the wedding. 'Mel told you, didn't she?'

'I think it was supposed to shame me, but how anyone could credit that I could come to your aid without even knowing where to find you is the mystery.'

'So back to square one again,' Lexy gathered in exasperation. 'You had my phone number—'

'I lost it. I don't know how.' Nic threw up his hands as she stared back at him with wide eyes, questioning such a well-worn excuse. 'But it *does* happen and unfortunately, *very* unfortunately in our case, it happened to me and I never got your surname or the name of the company you worked for or anything else which could have identified you.'

Lexy glanced away from his lean, darkly handsome features again. Now that she considered it, she could not recall giving him her full name or any other details. They had both been very laid-back in that line and she still remembered asking for his name and it was only because of that and his status that she had easily contrived to identify him and his workplace.

His dark eyes were suddenly serious. 'I had every intention of seeing you again.'

Oh, how she wanted to believe his excuse and that claim, like every other woman who had ever spent days and weeks waiting and totally expecting a call from a man because she had believed in him when she'd first met him. What kind of idiot would she be if she tried to believe in him again now? Or would faking trust she didn't feel be the gateway to peace between them?

'I'll *try* to believe that,' she breathed stiffly, stepping back from the brink of an endless tussle between them about who was lying about the past. Well, she already knew it wasn't her! But she didn't want to live in daily hostile exchanges with the man she had married. For wealth and security in the future, she reminded herself stubbornly, refusing to admit that she could have made a mistake marrying a stubborn-as-a-pig male who wouldn't tell the truth at the point of a gun! What other choices did she have?

None. No home, no job, no money. The daily struggle of poverty had meant that her children got less and she couldn't return to that with Ethan, Ezra and Lily when Nic had offered her the alternative. The seemingly *easy* alternative—the marriage—that was not quite so easy in practice.

The limo had left the road to pull up in front of a ginormous ultra-modern house. 'This is it?' she gasped, gaping at the black angled roof and the curvy walls.

'Yes.'

Without any warning, Nic waved a hand at the driver hovering to open the door beside her. 'Before we go into the house, is an agreement possible?'

'About…er…what?' she pressed anxiously, her smooth brow furrowing.

'Clearly, we have to leave the past behind us to share even the children,' Nic intoned gravely. 'Let's not make this marriage more difficult than it needs to be and risk subjecting our children to a bad atmosphere. For their benefit we should fake being together and acting happy and relaxed. I don't want my new relationship with them getting poisoned by *our* problems.'

Lexy went pink. 'I agree that would be a good idea, *but*—'

'Look on this as a holiday and on me as a friend and I will attempt to facilitate that view to the best of my ability.' Intense dark golden eyes held hers fast. The faint hint of cologne and male flared her nostrils. She loved the scent of him and her tummy danced with butterflies. This close to Nic she could barely think straight, and the label of friend was the very last one that she would have attached to her reaction to him.

'All right,' she agreed, amazed that after his denials he could turn everything on its head, think outside the box and come up with the suggestion of a truce, however temporary it might prove to be.

Was she only playing into his hands with her agreement? Papering over the cracks? But he was right, successfully sharing the house and the children, never mind their lives, entailed a certain harmony and right now they weren't anywhere near achieving that. How could he be so sensible and yet persist in acting as though she were the one lying about the past? That too was a question she deemed more wisely buried for the present. He had come up with a solution and she wasn't too proud to grasp an olive branch, particularly not when she had to think of the welfare of their three children.

Just as she was thinking that she noticed that Nic was stepping into the house, nodding to the house-keeper, bowing low. With a spurt of speed, she grabbed his elbow to hold him back. 'Take off your shoes,' she whispered as he bent his head down in turning round to find out what she was doing. 'Wearing them indoors is a big no-no here.'

'I forgot.' He bent down and removed them, fol-lowing her example of using the shoe rack provided at the lower level of the entrance hallway.

Relieved by his acceptance, Lexy moved into the house to speak to the housekeeper and introduce her to Nic. 'Nic, this is Kang Ji-Rae...' And she laughed. 'I think she's more excited about our kids than us. Triplets are popular here and more common.'

'You're going to be very useful here,' Nic told her.

Lexy laughed again as one of the nannies came in holding Lily and her daughter held out her arms to her father for the first time. His smile was huge as he lifted her, delighted by the invitation. Lexy grabbed Ethan, and Ezra started crying, and it was a little while then until they got the babies settled again with a selec-tion of toys and snacks. The babies had been incred-ibly good for babies whose whole routine had been disrupted by travel, Lexy informed Nic defensively.

'I thought they were marvellous during the flight,' he opined with a shrug.

'Only because they were in a private jet and they weren't restricted to a seat for most of the journey. We were very lucky.'

'Lucky to have them,' Nic chipped in as he re-arranged Ezra's bricks for his son to knock down again. 'They're happy babies. Considering that you were alone coping with them, you've done a terrific job.'

An uncertain smile of surprise curved Lexy's tense lips. 'Thanks.'

Reaching out, he closed his hand over her curled fingers. 'Relax, *chriso mou*,' he urged.

Feeling a prickling sensation spreading from her wrist with only that casual touch, she gently tugged her hand free again. 'Where are we sleeping?' she asked as the babies were pretty settled in and quite content.

'I'm afraid that didn't work out quite as I planned,' Nic murmured flatly, evidently having already established that reality while she was occupied with their children, faint colour flaring over his high cheekbones, accentuating the brilliance of his dark-as-night eyes.

'Meaning?' she prompted with assurance because she could tell embarrassment when she saw it.

'I assumed there would be enough rooms here for us to sleep separately but that is apparently not the case,' Nic breathed stiffly. 'This nursery has been set up in the room I expected you to occupy. It has a communicating door with the master suite, where we have been placed together.'

'We can manage,' she conceded grudgingly, belatedly foreseeing the intimacies she had expected to avoid with him. 'Let's hope it's a big bed.'

It was an enormous bed. Even for a male of Nic's imposing physique, it would be a challenge to accidentally bump into him in that amount of space, Lexy thought with relief. Because here he was, not doing a single thing to attract her, neither verbally nor physically, and the attraction still looked like a wall she couldn't bust down. That was life, she told herself, swings and roundabouts, and she had to learn how to handle life in close proximity with Nic Diamandis. Yes, and act like a platonic friend, so easy to say, so hard in reality if you were as fiercely attracted to someone as she was to him. She couldn't explain the source of that continuing attraction. No matter how hard she reminded herself of his transgressions, it was simply there as the air was there and the ground beneath her feet: always present, impossible to ignore.

'Dinner is at nine because the housekeeper didn't know when we would like to eat, but evening meals are generally scheduled at a much earlier hour here,' Lexy told him.

'Evidently, you promise to be an invaluable resource,' Nic remarked as he removed his suit jacket. 'What do I wear tomorrow to this first business meeting?'

'A black suit if you've brought one, accent on formal,' she told him a little breathless at the sight of the biceps moving below the fine fabric, only drawing her attention to the narrow cut of his waist and the lean flare of his hips and long, strong legs.

They parted into separate bathrooms. There might be only one master suite, but it was of lavish proportions. Lexy's clothing had already been hung in an equally separate dressing room and she selected a short, soft blue dress that was her version of casual formal.

Platonic—it was Nic's new inner placard for marital harmony, and she appeared from the bathroom as he was about to leave their room, slender and lithe as some sort of woodland sprite, he reflected abstractedly. And totally lovely in that weird female way where very little make-up and a brush through the hair could still make her look like a million dollars. Averting his attention, he went down to dinner.

Over dinner they made very polite conversation because both of them were tired, jet lag kicking in. Lexy excused herself first after enjoying only a light meal, the abundance of what they were offered more than her tummy could handle after such a long journey. She donned silky pyjamas from her huge collection of couture clothing, gifted by Nic prior to their marriage. Sliding into the vast bed, she rested her weary head down on a soft pillow.

And then the light by the bed flicked on again and she lowered her eyelids, determined not to react to Nic's proximity, because she was a big girl in terms of age and maturity and she wasn't about to make a fuss about the necessity of sharing a bedroom when they were a married couple. The bed shifted and gave a little with Nic's arrival. He doused the light. He was very quiet, very considerate of her presence, and for some reason it annoyed her, rather than soothing her.

'Are you exhausted?' she heard herself ask without any awareness that she was about to speak to him, which seemed impossible, but his existence in the same bed with her, even if she couldn't feel it, struck her just then as utterly unforgivable. He was this guy she had dared to marry, who had sex without really thinking about it and she couldn't forgive him for that. For the night before, the wedding night of her dreams, had turned into a fight instead.

'Not really. I dozed during the flight,' he admitted.

Gosh, wasn't it great to be a seasoned long-haul private-jet traveller? she thought nastily, and she knew she was being snippy and couldn't quell her tongue. 'Great not to be looking after three babies, wasn't it?'

'You weren't exclusively looking after our brood of babies either,' Nic pointed out smoothly as she sat up in a sudden movement to look down at him in the moonlight. 'That's why I hired three nannies.'

'I want to slap you right now,' Lexy confided shakily.

Nic slowly, gracefully, with a fluidity of motion that set her teeth even more on edge, sat up as well, the sheet dropping to his lean waist, shadow glimmering over his hard, muscular chest, picking out the swells and the hollows, every one of them in exactly the right place to drive a woman to madness. 'I get that, but I don't understand why,' he countered levelly.

'You don't understand why?' Lexy gasped in a rage with knotted fists. 'Last night you were in bed with me—'

'I'm not about to forget that.'

'Telling me that you dreamt of being with me like this, telling me that I was unbelievably sexy!' she whipped back fiercely.

'And it was all true,' Nic delivered like a man with a death wish, and she wanted to kill him stone-dead where he sat. 'One thing doesn't change…no matter *what* you say or do, I *still* want you.'

'How dare you?' she exclaimed, piling up his sins inside her brain like an avalanche ready to drown them both.

'I always dare,' Nic countered, stretching out a hand to smooth the tumbled hair from her cheekbone, to tuck it neatly behind one small ear, the brush of his very fingers setting up a chain of reaction through her body.

Her nipples strained and prickled under her light camisole, goose flesh sprang up on her exposed skin and her tummy danced with butterflies again while her lower regions, well, she didn't even want to think about the receptive warmth gathering there. That she could be that weak, *that* susceptible to him, inflamed her.

'*I* dare because you don't even try,' he murmured sibilantly.

And somehow it was either slap him or kiss him, and later she wouldn't comprehend what made her lean forward and seek his wide, sensual, thoroughly annoying mouth for herself. Nonetheless, she *did*. Warm lips brushing, a hand closing over her elbow to ease her closer, and she fell into that kiss like a snowflake on a summer day. Her anger melted into something else entirely, something that really didn't seem to matter in the height of her overwhelming response of that moment.

He could kiss. Every time he kissed her, she forgot how good it was, even if only the night before had been the last time. And that wasn't an excuse, because she was past making excuses when every fibre of her being urged her simply to connect with him again as though it had been months when it had been only hours. As his tongue took a subtle dance across the roof of her mouth before connecting with her own, she grabbed him with both hands and he closed both arms round her, tugging her closer until her breasts were crushed against his broad chest.

And then, in the midst of that passion, Nic pushed her back and gazed down at her with his stunning dark eyes glittering. 'I need to be certain that this is what *you* want.'

And that was it because all of a sudden she was back in her own head and body and just then it felt as though it would be yet another massive betrayal of pride and dignity to allow such closeness.

'It's not what I want,' she lied without hesitation.

Lexy lay back down, her body humming and pulsing like an engine that had geared up for a race. She didn't want to think, she refused to think beyond the reality that in the nicest possible way her husband had rejected her and she was back to wishing she could strike him stone dead.

Only that wasn't what she truly wanted either, she registered in growing dismay. She really didn't want anything bad to happen to Nic Diamandis. And why was that? As she mulled over that final thought, only exhaustion sent her to sleep.

CHAPTER EIGHT

As Nic and Lexy emerged from the lengthy business meeting, Nic was in a better mood with his bride. She had been a professional and businesslike interpreter for the duration and, while once or twice seeking clarity on some technical term from him, she had been confident and impressive. As they entered the lift together, he turned to her. 'What were you chatting about to the chairman at the end? He seemed very pleased.'

'I told him that we would be visiting Bongeun-sa Temple this afternoon and he was delighted that you are taking interest in culture here,' she explained lightly.

'And are we truly planning to make this trip?' Nic enquired, angling up one sardonic brow.

'Obviously.' Her eyes assailed his, her lovely face serious. 'It wouldn't do not to go as you'll probably be asked for your impression of the site at your next meeting. I've been before on several school outings and it's a lovely relaxing place, right in the heart of the city.'

'Did you also mention that this is our honeymoon?'

Lexy went pink. 'That would be too personal for sharing but I would imagine that the chairman is already aware. This company is his life's work and although he does not have a family to pass it on to, he wants to sell to a businessman he regards as good, and the "traditional family man with children" image will serve you well here.'

Nic nodded, appreciating how astute she was, how efficient. How that bled into her less presentable flaws he had yet to discover, he brooded.

They returned to the house for lunch and spent some time with their children before heading back out to the Buddhist temple, which had an amazing location, set as it was in the very heart of the towering glass city skyscrapers, perfectly preserved on a hillside filled with vast and ancient trees.

'I would have brought the children but there's too many steps for the pram,' she explained rather guiltily.

'The house has a massive garden. Easier to entertain three babies on the spot,' Nic quipped, staring down at her as she stood in the shade, her silky hair catching a flickering strand of sunlight and gleaming gold, her eyes translucent in colour. His hand came down on her shoulder and he felt her tense as he bent his dark head.

In a sudden movement, Lexy twisted away just as an elderly monk came down the steps with a wooden staff, studying them as he passed with a frown. 'I'm sorry,' she said, her lips tingling as though he had actually touched them with his. He hadn't, but there had been a certain heat in his gaze that had spelled out his intention.

Nic had straightened, strong tension etched in his strong jawline. Dismayed, Lexy reached for his hand and laced her fingers through his. 'Out of respect, *this* is as close to friendly as we can get as this is a sacred site,' she proffered apologetically while wondering why she was bothering to explain, because surely he should not even be *trying* to kiss her! She fell off that mental high horse as soon as she recalled kissing him the night before in their bed and her face turned red as fire.

An unexpected laugh of understanding was wrenched from Nic and he glanced at her. 'Relax, *glykia mou*…you're as red as a traffic light but I'm not on the brink of dragging you into the bushes *yet*. Who knows what condition or mood I'll be in within another couple of days?' he teased.

As she attempted to release his hand, his fingers merely tightened their hold and she gave up before an unseemly tussle could occur. Nic definitely didn't appreciate being told what he could and could not do with a woman, she registered, particularly one to whom he was married. And she supposed that, even in a slightly twisty way, she could understand his reasoning.

After all, what had *he* gained from their marriage?

Full access to Ethan, Ezra and Lily and legal rights over them. Mel, ever the lawyer, had ensured that Lexy was well acquainted with those facts before she'd reached the altar. Even so, Nic had given up far more than Lexy. He had enjoyed total freedom, unfettered by anyone or anything, and he had surrendered that freedom to marry her.

Lexy, on the other hand, had gone from rags to riches and had escaped much of the daily slog of raising three demanding babies. In short, prior to their marriage, she had had *no* freedom to lose. So how did Nic feel now, stuck with a platonic partner in his bed? He was a man who was probably accustomed to enjoying sex whenever or wherever that desire took him. He was not used to sudden celibacy being forced on him.

'I have a question,' Nic murmured as they slowly climbed the steep steps of the temple.

'What do you want to know?' she asked, removing her footwear to enter the shrine.

'Why did you sleep with me on our wedding night?' Nic enquired, smooth as glass.

In the act of bowing to the custodian greeting them, Lexy winced, gritted her teeth and flushed miserably while wishing that he had chosen a more private moment for such an inquiry.

But then Nic could be very impatient. It had been a struggle for him to talk at the slow, measured pace of the elderly chairman and show that deference for age that was expected in Korea. Now a thought had occurred to him and he had plunged impulsively right in with it, even though the surroundings were inappropriate. Annoyed by his candid question and put on the spot, Lexy simply ignored it while inside the temple cymbals clashed, small bells rang and soft chanting began. He dealt her a fulminating appraisal and she ignored that as well, watching while he paced restively back and forth through the vacant space behind her.

Lexy's temper raced up through her like a rocket ship. He only listened when he wanted to listen, only talked when he wished to, and had pushed her away when she had given him considerable encouragement the night before. It didn't matter what she did, somehow he *always* found fault! Her teeth ground together and her chin came up, anger darkening her more usually calm gaze.

Without a word she joined him again to walk back to the car.

'You've got nothing to say to me...*at all*?' Nic shot at her in a decidedly scornful undertone.

Lexy felt like a pot on a stove ready to boil over and she couldn't contain that indignation. Whipping round on a quiet curve of the path, she breathed, 'I slept with you because an unconsummated marriage can be set aside as invalid in some circumstances. And naturally, when we're going for a divorce, it wouldn't be in *my* best interests to risk that. Happy now? Gold-digger wife right here!'

As she stared defiantly up at him, Nic's darkly handsome features froze and he lost colour below his olive skin. Sudden shame and mortification engulfed Lexy as they walked back in tense silence. What a thing to say to him when they were supposed to be doing the mature thing and sticking to a civilised truce! Why did Nic Diamandis make her act like a volatile teenager? It took a great deal to make Lexy lose her temper and he kept on bringing out that side of her and she hated it! She had lied to make a point, to save her pride, to pretend that she was cunning and mercenary. She had preferred him to believe that rather than the unlovely truth that she was simply a pushover for him.

'Did your best friend of a lawyer tell you that you had to sleep with me at least *once*?'

'No, Mel didn't, actually. I read it some place a year or two back,' she admitted wearily, relieved to tell the truth about something. 'I don't even know if it's still a legal requirement these days.'

She stepped into the luxury vehicle that glided next to the kerb to pick them up and sidled along to the far end of the rear seat. Chagrin held her fast and then just as suddenly as she had lost her temper, the anger was gone and she breathed out slowly. 'I was lying,' she told him reluctantly. 'I was annoyed with you and so I lied. That was wrong, particularly when we're trying to work out how to navigate this marriage peaceably.'

Nic was stunned by that wholly unexpected speech, that fierce quality of sincerity that powered her and the sheer honesty it carried. Brilliant dark eyes locked to her flushed and unhappy profile. 'You're admitting that you were lying?'

'Why wouldn't I? The reason I gave—about an unconsummated marriage—was untrue and hurtful as a motivation and I shouldn't have said it,' Lexy conceded heavily. 'I slept with you because I wanted you and for no other reason.'

'You still want me?'

'Haven't I admitted that already?' she exclaimed in extreme self-consciousness.

'I only pushed you away last night because I wasn't sure you knew what you wanted from me,' Nic confessed, disconcerting Lexy as well with his frankness. 'And I didn't want to risk screwing things up with you again.'

'Oh...' Lexy felt hot and uncomfortable, probably, she reflected ruefully, because she wasn't used to discussing anything to do with sex. And the law of averages being what it was, she had landed the guy who would say anything and talk about it even in the equivalent of a church!

Nic muttered a Greek curse under his breath. He felt weirdly light-headed for an instant. Lexy *still* wanted him. No doubt it was pleasing him to hear that so much because he burned for her every time he looked at her. And he reckoned that he looked at her and thought about sex at least sixty times an hour. No woman had ever had that effect on him before and he was seriously hoping that that fixated hunger died away soon because it wasn't easy to tolerate in a relationship as fractured as theirs was. It had been even less easy to tolerate when he had been unable to find her, he reminded himself darkly. He *needed* to get that sexual infatuation out of his system before the divorce happened. Of course, getting a divorce didn't need to be set in stone, he reasoned. That was something that could only be decided between the two of them and who knew how their marriage would develop in the coming months?

All of a quiver, literally, because Lexy couldn't get that disturbingly intimate conversation out of her head, she returned to the house with him and they spent time with the children in the nursery on the floor. Ezra adored Nic, crawling straight to him, grabbing at his hands to play his favourite game of standing up, because Ezra was desperate to stand and walk. Ethan came more slowly to him, wary, grasping his hands and then bouncing with all his exuberant energy and laughing out loud with sweet baby vigour. Lily came to Lexy, a calmer personality like her mother, and rested on her lap sleepily. She was always quicker to tire than her brothers. Lexy cuddled her daughter with a heart full to overflowing.

'Dinner is set for six-thirty because I said we don't mind eating earlier,' she told him softly. 'I didn't consult you—'

'No, that's fine with me. It's been a long day,' Nic conceded, tugging loose his tie and undoing his collar, sculpted stubbled jawline clenching to throw his flawlessly chiselled features into prominence, accentuating his high cheekbones, his straight ebony brows, his aristocratic nose and wide, perfect mouth.

And she thought, how do I handle this, this unbearable longing, this hunger that comes out of nowhere and just seizes hold of me? He looked as delicious as a long cold drink on a too hot day. Swallowing hard, she turned away as they entered their room, heading straight for the dressing room to choose a fresh outfit. She chose a slim pink sheath dress and changed inside the dressing room, not wishing to hand out signals she wasn't sure she wished to follow up.

Returning to the bedroom, she learned that Nic suffered from no such inhibitions. Naked, bronzed and muscular, Nic was getting dressed too and she drifted straight back out of the bedroom and downstairs to wait for him. How did she traverse such intimacies now? Certainly, she shouldn't be watching him the way she did, *unless…* Why shouldn't she want him when she was married to him? Would a man think twice about watching his wife undress?

They ate a meal of so many dishes and courses, arranged across the tabletop in Korean banquet style, that she had to name it all for Nic. He sampled *bulgogi*, thin beef marinated in sweet soy sauce, *ssam*, grilled meat wrapped in vegetable leaves, *samgyetang*, ginseng chicken soup, *gimbap*, round rolls of rice with savoury extras, fish, rice and noodles. *Kimchi*, pickled vegetables, she explained, appeared at every meal. She suggested that she take him out to sample street food some evening and offered him hints for how he should behave when he dined out later in the week with the chairman at a renowned restaurant.

As she finished the cookie provided for dessert, Nic stood up and closed a hand over hers. 'Let's go to bed,' he murmured lazily.

Lexy reddened because it was still very early. 'It's only—'

'And this is our honeymoon,' he reminded her smoothly.

As he pressed her upstairs, she shed her insecurity. He wanted her and she wanted him. There was absolutely no reason why they should not explore that connection more. He was kissing her long before they reached their bedroom and she was grabbing handfuls of his shirtfront in her eagerness to reach actual skin.

'You're wearing far too many clothes,' she told him.

'So are you,' he said, closing the bedroom door, peeling off his jacket, ripping off his tie and his shirt with an urgency that thrilled her.

'It wasn't supposed to be like this,' she framed without much vigour.

Nic spun her round, ran down her zip and the dress fell to her feet. 'But it *is*...'

While she kicked off her shoes, Nic stripped off his clothes and she couldn't take her eyes off that lean, muscular physique of his and the heated ache at the core of her merely gathered strength. With new decisiveness, Lexy reached behind herself to undo her bra and cast it off, wriggling her hips to shed her knickers. Even while she was doing such things, she was marvelling at the new confidence he gave her. But then a guy viewing her body with the same appreciation he might have awarded a goddess *was* pretty encouraging, she thought, helpless to resist such silent flattery.

He came down on the bed with her, all urgent and aroused and reaching for her, and her heart was hammering so hard she was out of breath, losing herself in the allure of his hungry kiss, the crushing of her lips by his, the sensual exploration of his tongue that sent sensation winging through her whole body.

'I've never wanted anyone the way I want you,' Nic growled, spreading her across the bed to work a slow steady passage down over her slender curves, long fingers touching, teasing, penetrating, watching as her spine rose and a gasp escaped her. 'And I really couldn't wait any longer tonight.'

He made her feel like the most beautiful woman in the world and when she looked at him his sheer gorgeousness almost overpowered her because, realistically, Nic Diamandis had been her fantasy from the first moment she saw him. She ran admiring fingers through his thick black hair, moaned as he found a raspberry-pink straining nipple with his devouring mouth and moaned even louder when he traced the most sensitive spot of all and shifted his attention there with keen concentration. Her first orgasm hit her like a train roaring down a hill and, moments later, he tilted her up and thrust into her slow and deep.

'Ah…' she sighed because as her body so welcomed the invasion of his, it felt impossibly good and little quivers of response eddied through her pelvis.

He flexed his hips and changed speed with a grunt of pleasure as she lifted up to him. From that point, self-control fled Lexy, if it had ever existed. Excitement vanquished discipline and drove every thought out of her head. Sensation was cascading through her willing body in a dam burst of elation. Breath caught in her throat, her heart racing, she was flying higher and higher, particularly after he slid off her, flipped her over and grabbed her hips to raise her again and drove back into her in that new position. She hit an explosive climax right then again, pleasure surging afresh when he kept going, jolting her with ever deeper thrusts. A shriek she muffled in the pillows erupted from her as she reached the plateau again and finally flopped down, convinced she would never move again.

'That was…' Words escaped her.

'Wild. You like it fast and hard…as do I,' Nic informed her, words not evading him.

Lexy grimaced into the pillows and flipped over again. 'Just don't ask me to comment afterwards,' she mumbled awkwardly. 'This is all still too new to me for me to feel comfy talking about it.'

'Still?' he queried.

'Well, when on earth could I have had the freedom to do this with anyone else?' she shot at him irritably.

Nic pulled her close, tossing the rumpled sheet over her, leaning back, feeling fairly pleased with the world in general because she was simply amazing in bed. And she was his wife, something of a sobering recollection, he registered. His wife for at least a year, maybe even longer. Well, there was no reason why they shouldn't enjoy their time together. Temporary truce for a temporary marriage.

But a thought crept in… A divorce would mean Lexy and his children moving into their own accommodation. Like that chateau in France Angeliki had had the bad taste to mention. He wondered what he was going to do about his half-sister. At the wedding she had behaved a little like a jealous girlfriend and he didn't want Lexy to end up in Angeliki's line of fire. It would have been so much easier if Angeliki hadn't tried to seduce him that night. If that hadn't happened, he would have felt able to tell her immediately that they shared a father. At least if he told her the truth about their blood relationship, she would back off and stop acting so possessive, he reasoned, resolving to move ahead with telling his best friend the truth to stop her interfering in his life.

He pictured Lexy as lady of the chateau in France. She wouldn't be on the single shelf for very long, he ruminated, growing increasingly less relaxed as that reality sank in on him hard. He was appalled by the idea of her with another man. In fact, the concept almost made him feel sick. As for the children moving out from under his roof and a potential stepfather pushing his way in? Well, those possibilities held no appeal either. He released his breath in a pent-up rush. There was no need to think about all that stuff now. Presumably a few months down the road he would feel differently.

After all, there wasn't any way he would tie himself down for any longer to a liar, was there? No guy in his right mind would do that.

'I suppose I should get up. It's only half eight,' Lexy lamented.

Nic locked both arms round her, trapping her without even thinking about it. 'No. I have plans for you.'

'Really?' Looking at him upside down, Lexy's eyes widened.

'Yes, we stay in bed and use the opportunity,' he murmured, moving her onto the bed beside him and claiming her swollen mouth with his again.

CHAPTER NINE

NIC SUPPRESSED A SIGH, reluctant to move as he eased back from his wife's sleeping body. Obviously, the honeymoon idyll had to end, and he had to get back to work. For the first time in twenty-nine years he had been lazy. More than three weeks of sheer unpardonable sloth, the fast-track week in Korea, followed by two weeks on the island of Faros, living in his late father's monstrous gilded palace.

Sightseeing followed by sun, sea, sand. *And sex.* He covered Lexy's slender thigh with a large towel because he didn't want her to burn when the sun moved. Vaulting upright, he adjusted the overhead canopy to ensure that she remained in the shade. Below the giant lounger the sand was churned up, awash with buckets, spades and Nic's first attempt since childhood at a sandcastle, all the evidence of the triplets' presence earlier. Tears and tiredness had sent them back up to the house with their nannies for a nap.

Lexy's sheaf of golden hair was tangled, her face composed, her slender little body relaxed. Something tugged hard in his chest and he breathed out heavily.

He told himself that it was good that he was leaving her for a day. They needed a break, they needed to let the rest of the world in, only it wouldn't help him to reach a decision about what to do about her and his marriage. Keeping the truce they had agreed, but not confronting her afresh, was *killing* him because Nic was like a dog with a bone when anything angered him and he couldn't let it go, no matter how hard he tried.

His lean, strong features were tense, his frown darkening in tenor. The marriage that was never supposed to be a proper marriage and the honeymoon that happened purely by accident. By accident? *Theos mou*, wasn't he a little too mature to be choosing an excuse of that kind? Lexy was the wife he had never planned to have, who had somehow become a real wife. She was thicker than thieves with his mother and his sister-in-law, Gigi. As for his grandmother, Electra, who rarely complimented any woman, his yaya had told him he had done exceptionally well in choosing Lexy as a life partner. And his brother, Jace, loved the fact that their wives got on like a house on fire.

But this afternoon he had to fly into Athens and discover the nature of the 'urgent personal matter' that had prompted his London office manager, Leigh, to fly to Greece for a confidential meeting. Leigh didn't fuss over the small stuff. Leigh was level-headed. Someone on his staff must have screwed up very badly and Leigh was blaming herself, he surmised, or perhaps Leigh had developed some ghastly serious illness, which she wanted kept secret. What else could it be?

He was fond of the older woman, who had once worked for his father and who was more efficient than anyone else in either office in London or Athens. She managed his staff with quiet assurance, managed *him* to some degree too, he conceded with wry amusement, prompting him to take a break when he worked too many hours, sending in food to sustain him, and she guarded him from unwelcome callers like a Rottweiler.

'You should have woken me up!' Lexy scolded, catching up with him on the path up from the beach, panting slightly at the gradient. 'You're leaving, aren't you?'

'I hope to make it back for dinner,' Nic admitted, grabbing her hand to physically pull her up the last few feet. 'But don't wait up for me if I'm late.'

He strode into the echoing hall where a litter of tiny sandy sandals almost tripped him up. The triplets were walking but some better than others. Ethan still wobbled like a tiny drunk. Lily was the most sure-footed, but she had taken a vehement dislike to sand. Ezra was full of glee at his own prowess and loved to get his feet wet.

Nic smiled, loving the lack of order that was gradually invading his father's once very grand property.

Lexy had changed things. The staff were more relaxed, the structure of the household less rigid, the
meals more casual and everybody was happier, in-
cluding himself. He, however, was no less rigid in
his moral outlook than he had always been, he acknowledged uneasily as he stepped into the shower.
He could not abide dishonesty. He could not commit
to a woman who had lied to him. How could he ever
trust her?

The most likely scenario, he had decided, was that
Lexy had met another man after that night in Yorkshire. Perhaps she had doubted the paternity of her
children at that point and very probably she had not
wished to contact Nic and pull him back into her life
just then. What else was he supposed to think when
he was continually seeking justification for her long
silence and even more dubious claims? After all, he
knew that she could never have visited his office without him being informed of the fact, even if it was after
the event. Phone calls? Leigh would've consulted him.
Letters? They would have arrived on his desk.

Nic was in a dark mood, Lexy thought, emerging
from her own shower, for once blessing the separate facilities of the huge master bedroom suite they
occupied together. But he wouldn't talk about what
was on his mind, even if she was convinced that she
already knew.

After all, wasn't she worrying too? Here they were,

married and with three kids, and the 'faking the marriage' idea had never even got off the ground in reality. Somehow their relationship had become genuine, the scorching physical chemistry between them too powerful to overcome or ignore. That had been their first mistake, the mistake of total intimacy, she recognised, but the biggest mistake of all was that she had fallen for him again. Absolutely, totally and for ever fallen in love with Nic Diamandis for the second time. And why not? Wasn't he still her fantasy guy? Her perfect guy with one major drawback: he didn't trust her, didn't believe in her and as a result he never talked about anything with her that might be happening more than two days in advance.

She sensed that he was almost always right on the edge of walking out of their messy relationship. And why did he stay? Oh, that was a very easy question to answer. He stayed because he adored Ethan, Ezra and Lily. Once he ended their marriage, he would be deprived of daily access to his sons and his daughter.

Nic emerged from his dressing room, fully clad in a sharply cut black suit teamed with a silver-grey shirt and tie. As always, he looked amazing. He was every inch the tech billionaire who had recently acquired a legendary South Korean computer firm that would ensure his empire maintained an even sharper edge in the development stakes.

'I've been thinking that I may stay on for a few days in Athens,' Nic told her quietly. 'It's time I caught up with work. We'll be returning to London soon anyway.'

Her tummy shifted queasily, a hollow opening inside her heart. 'I could come with you,' she pointed out and hated herself for stating the obvious.

'I take too many breaks when you're around,' he parried drily. 'But I'll miss the kids.'

Only he would not miss her, that obvious qualification of his coming to her mind and wounding. He hadn't said that he would miss *her*. Maybe all she was to Nic Diamandis was convenient sex on tap and, when required, a mother to his children. Well, tough cookie, she thought in sudden defiance. She was worth more than that!

As her husband strode on downstairs, she watched him head for the helipad where his pilot was awaiting his arrival. Just as quickly and noisily he was gone in the helicopter with its distinctive Diamandis logo, up into the air and en route to Athens. And was she planning to be here waiting obediently for his now unspecified date of return? No, to hell with that idea!

She had to be proactive when it came to her own life. She lived in a fake marriage that already had a specified end date. But Nic wasn't happy and neither was she. Returning to London, asserting her independence, made sense because he wasn't going to be part of her life for ever anyway. She needed to move on, make plans for the future, lay down some solid foundations. For the past month, all she had done, she conceded with squirming reluctance, was lay down for *him*. And romanticise absolutely everything they had shared, which, in the circumstances, was unforgivable. Her fingers worked nervously at the gold necklace she wore, a designer piece he had bought her on Corfu on one of their days out on Jace's yacht.

She remembered the look in his eyes as he'd clasped it round her throat, that way he had of looking at her as if she were the only woman in the world, the hundred per cent attention always focused on her. It was a kind of charisma Nic Diamantis had, she reasoned, that ability to make a woman feel special even if she wasn't, but ultimately it *hurt*. Every hour he spent with her hurt because no gesture, no act of passion, no tender words ultimately meant anything to him. He was only keeping the stupid truce, keeping her content because a contented woman didn't make waves.

That awareness in mind, she rang Jace's wife, Gigi, conscious that they were flying back to London that very afternoon, to ask if she could accompany them.

'Didn't Nic ask you to go with him to Athens?' her sister-in-law asked in surprise.

Lexy's cheeks burned red as the heart of a fire in mortification. 'No, and he's not sure when he's coming back either so I thought I might as well head to London now in advance. I know you're leaving today and I was hoping you could give us a lift…all of us, the kids and the nannies.'

'Of course we can, but I'll check with Jace first,' Gigi completed more slowly, clearly thinking through to try and guess what was motivating Lexy.

'Do you think he'll say no?' Lexy asked before she could bite back the nervous question.

'No, Jace keeps his own counsel, but I assume you have your reasons,' Gigi responded calmly. 'And in any case, if you want to head to London today you could make your own arrangements, but you might as well travel with company. We can wrangle kids together.'

While Lexy was planning her departure from the island, Nic was entering his Athens head office, lifting his hand to greet familiar faces without pausing while being assured that Leigh awaited him upstairs in his office. He strode into the sunlit room, apprehension tensing his muscles as he scanned the older woman with her dark hair worn in an elegant chignon and her steady blue eyes.

'Firstly,' Leigh began in an anxious undertone, 'I want to tender my resignation, sir—'

'What on earth…?' Nic breathed with a frown, wrong-footed by that startling opening to their meeting.

'I made a bad decision because I chose to trust someone close to you and when I've finished explaining myself and my actions, you will be very angry with me,' she assured him unhappily. Moving forward, she laid a slender folder down on his desk. 'I kept records of everything though.'

'Someone close to me?' Nic was already prompting, ebony brows pleated, because very few people were close to him outside his family. He had long conserved his independence and ensured that his judgement was unaffected by others. It was probably, he conceded, the only preference he had copied from his father's chosen operational secretive mode in business.

'Miss Bouras,' Leigh declared, disconcerting him even more as she stepped forward.

'Angeliki has nothing to do with any aspect of my business,' he said defensively.

'This is personal, confidential,' Leigh reminded him sadly. 'And I was the fool who listened to her and followed her advice. Look at this first...'

Nic froze and grasped the phone she was extending to study the photograph showing on the screen and disbelief assailed him. It was a picture of Lexy chopping vegetables in his kitchen in Yorkshire that long ago night. A photo he had believed that he had taken when she was unawares and had later searched for but failed to find on his phone—he had assumed that he had done it too quickly and it hadn't taken. 'Where did you get this photo from?'

'Miss Bouras gave it to me for identification purposes,' the older woman explained.

A sinking sensation hit Nic's stomach. 'Why would she do that? *Identification?*'

'Miss Bouras came to see me. Almost two years ago. She explained that you had a very persistent female stalker causing you an awful lot of grief.'

'A...a stalker?' Nic exclaimed in disbelief. 'I've never had a stalker in my life... This woman... Lexy is my wife!'

'Yes, and I'm afraid I only realised that she was an official part of your life when I saw the pictures of your wedding online,' Leigh admitted with a grimace. 'But I believed what Miss Bouras told me and I did as she asked.'

'What did she ask you to do?' Nic shot at her in a harsh undertone.

'To protect you from this woman, this supposedly obnoxious stranger trying to force herself into your life. She said that you were greatly embarrassed by the situation and trying to handle the problem discreetly. I could imagine you reacting that way to a female stalker...' Leigh muttered ruefully. 'You wouldn't want a fuss or any scenes at the office.'

'Leigh... I've never *had* a stalker!' Nic repeated forcefully. 'I can't credit that Angeliki approached you with this ridiculous story.'

Leigh looked grave. 'She did, sir, and she was very specific in her advice and instructions. She told me to destroy any letters that arrived, but I kept them as I assumed there would be a court case eventually and that you would need them as evidence. I noted down the phone calls and any visits that the young lady made.'

'The young lady being my *wife*?' Nic almost whispered, his stomach turning over sickly. Letters, *visits*, exactly as Lexy had claimed.

'It wasn't until I saw the wedding photos that I understood that I had made a very grave error in listening to Miss Bouras and trusting her word, rather than approaching you direct to discuss her instructions with you. You would scarcely marry a stalker.'

'Thank you for that understanding at least,' Nic muttered, raking an abstracted hand through his thick black hair while true comprehension began to sink in hard as a hammer blow to the head. Indeed, he felt as though he had been body-slammed against a brick wall and the stuffing had been knocked out of him. He was in shock.

He was already thinking back to the phone number that had disappeared from his phone. He hadn't thought much about the photo, only that he had taken it in haste while she had been unaware and that perhaps it hadn't taken, after all. But only one person ever knew the current password he had on his phone, his friend from childhood, Angeliki. Only one person had ever had free access to his phone and she had evidently used it to ensure that he couldn't contact Lexy.

And lo and behold, that was the same person, the *only* person, he had innocently told about Lexy. He had returned from Yorkshire the same day that Angeliki had finally decided to take his calls and he had been so high on that time with Lexy that he had mentioned to his half-sister that he had met 'someone', an important *someone*, whom he had named and described and waxed lyrical about.

Theos mou, what an idiot he had been! Thinking back to that period, he knew that only a complete fool would have talked about another woman to a woman he had recently rejected. Only by then he had already been thinking of his best friend as his half-sister, a safe confidante to his mind, if not hers.

'My worst recollection is of instructing the security men to show your pregnant wife-to-be down to the street,' Leigh almost whispered, her blue eyes shining with tears of regret. 'I felt dreadful about that even at the time but I thought… I thought it was my duty, my job to protect you from annoyance and unnecessary drama. I believed Miss Bouras. I knew you trusted her and I trusted her as well until I saw those pictures of your wedding. Then I realised that I had to come forward and speak up. Look, I've already taken up enough of your time and I can see that you're rather taken aback by all this—'

'Try…shocked speechless,' Nic corrected in a roughened undertone. 'But it's not your fault. I trusted Miss Bouras too. You cannot resign over this matter. I will explain all this…*somehow* to my wife. I will deal with the consequences. It is my responsibility.'

'Every call your wife made to our London office was logged and every letter is contained in the file, sir. The letters are unopened, of course,' the older woman proffered uncomfortably, indicating the file lying on his desk. 'I'm sorry about all this stuff. I know you don't like it.'

But Angeliki did, Nic reflected darkly. Angeliki thrived on drama, would have enjoyed coming into his office, telling her lies, ensuring that not a single person on his staff would give credence to Lexy, indeed would instead treat her like a stalker, a woman trying to force herself into his life where she was unwanted and unwelcome. And he felt seriously nauseous again when he recalled how very badly he had wanted to hear from Lexy twenty-odd months ago. It was as though his life had suddenly been rolled back in time and he was reliving what he would have felt then. Furious anger filled him. He knew that he had to see Angeliki first, had to confront her and finally tell her that they were siblings.

Once more refusing to accept Leigh's resignation, telling her that she had been as deceived in her trust of Angeliki as he had long been, Nic left the office to visit Angeliki's penthouse apartment.

Angeliki's housekeeper answered the door and ushered him into the airy reception room where her mistress was lying along a couch with a magazine, wearing a silk teddy below a sheer robe that she didn't bother to close as she sprang up, a huge smile lifting her beautiful face. 'Nic...always a welcome visitor.'

'Put something on,' he urged brusquely. 'You're not going to like me much after I've finished talking to you.'

In an exaggerated movement, Angeliki tied the sash on the robe, too proud of her long, shapely body to be pleased about hiding it.

'This is about Lexy, my wife.' Nic felt the need to attach that possessive label, noting how the blonde's face tightened. 'The moment I told you about her, you conducted a campaign to prevent her from coming back into my life.'

Angeliki raised a pencilled brow. 'Of course I did. I had to prevent you from doing something stupid because you were acting like a teenager about her. I've never seen you like that over a woman.'

'And clearly it was very stupid of me to confide in you. You broke into my phone, didn't you? Stole the photo, blocked her number, did every rotten thing you could to ensure I *couldn't* see her again!'

'Because you were about to make a *huge* mistake! I'm your best friend. I protected you from yourself.'

'I didn't need protecting. I'm an adult and far from innocent.'

'You were infatuated for the first time in your life!' Angeliki sliced in with a cutting edge of venom. 'You didn't know what you were doing. *Theos mou*, you had only parted from her a couple of hours and you were already agonising over whether or not you would look desperate if you phoned her!'

'You cut off someone who was important to me and, even worse, you left her no means to contact me when she needed my support because she was pregnant. So, no, Angeliki, I have nothing to thank you for. You deprived me of seeing my children coming into this world, you deprived me of times with the four of them that I will never get back!' Nic raged at her, out of all patience with her drivel. 'My office manager has told me that you gave her Lexy's photo and said that she was a stalker.'

His half-sister backed off a few steps and grimaced. 'Oh, she's told you about that. I was hoping that my intervention wouldn't come out for a while.'

'You don't screw up other people's lives like this,' Nic breathed rawly. 'It's unpardonable. Why did you do it? Were you jealous that I wanted her and not you?'

'Oh, don't be silly. I don't *do* jealousy.' Angeliki actually snorted with scornful laughter at that accusation. 'I've never cared about any of the women you've been with! But she got in my way and I don't let anyone do that to me.'

Nic lifted a lean brown hand. 'News update, Angeliki. Now I'm *in your way* too and if you ever get in hers again, I will ruin you! I don't know why you think Lexy was in your way when you and I weren't even seeing each other.'

'Because you *married* her!' Angeliki launched back at him in angry interruption, her dark eyes hard and cold. 'That was *my* place you gave her, not hers! Together we could be the new power couple in Greece. You were always meant to be mine, Nic, but I had to wait for you to grow up and see that we *belong* together—'

'We don't, and never could be together,' Nic incised with the icy bite of finality. 'Not only do I not want you in that way, but you are my half-sister. We share the same father.'

Angeliki backed off several feet, shock etched in her fine features. 'That's not possible. My mother always hated your father for the way he bullied mine.'

'It happened between them and you are the result, accept it.' Nic shrugged, not in a sympathetic mood. 'The legacy that made you an unexpected heiress came from my father's private coffers, not from some distant relative. Argus paid his dues in that line.'

Angeliki stared back at him in horror, as if her whole world were falling down on top of her. 'That's not possible...because that means that when I got into *your* bed—'

'Nothing happened,' Nic reminded her shortly.

'And how long have you known about this?'

'Since a letter was given to me after my father's will was read. I was going to tell you then, but the bedroom episode had recently occurred and I didn't want to make the announcement until the dust had settled on that.'

'You're my brother,' Angeliki said queasily. 'That toad, Jace, who won't give me the time of day, is my brother too.'

'And you and I are not friends any more and never will be again,' Nic framed coldly. 'Not after what you did to Lexy. Are you even aware that your lies about her being a stalker led to her being thrown out of my office building when she was heavily pregnant? I suspect you don't care.'

'You're right there!' Angeliki lashed back at him bitterly, dark eyes hard and hollow, reminding him unpleasantly of his late father. 'I don't give a damn. The blasted Diamandis family looks after itself and nobody else. I wish you'd had sex with me that night because it would have made you feel dirty and you're such a clean, decent guy. You were *never* for me!'

'That's good.' Turning on his heel, Nic strode out of her apartment with a sense of relief. He still had to see his mother, bring her up to date with the Angeliki situation, but he had had enough emotional drama for one day.

He had, he accepted, wrecked his relationship with Lexy from day one of their reunion. His principles had got the better of him. He had been blind, judgemental and intolerant. He had wanted Lexy to be that one perfect ideal woman without flaws. And fancy this, she truly *was*. He was the one with all the flaws, the guy who had learned he couldn't trust anyone at a very young age.

Not his father, who had once rammed him head first into a wall for irritating him as a toddler and put him into hospital. Not his mother, who had always put his father first and made excuses or lied for Argus, regardless of what he did. Not the string of women chasing him for his wealth, his status or even the right to stand beside him in a photo and reap that fleeting fame. And not even the one close friend he had ever had, Angeliki, who had clearly been determined to marry him from early on right up until she discovered that she was a blood relation. He also saw in her that, of all three Diamandis siblings, she resembled Argus the most with her cold, calculating, unscrupulous nature. What she wanted, she got, and she didn't care how she had to go about getting it. He had been learning to trust his older brother, but they had only got to know each other after their father's death, and he had retained his wariness about letting anyone come close.

By the time Jace phoned him to tell him that he was taking Lexy and the triplets to London with him, Nic was hitting a bottle of whiskey hard and hating himself. He had hurt his wife *again* and she was leaving him. It was exactly what he deserved...to lose her and his children.

CHAPTER TEN

'MY FATHER COULDN'T leave the London town house to Nic because it was mine according to the terms of the Diamandis trust. So, shortly before he died, he bought one directly across the street in the same square to leave to your husband.'

'How very convenient,' Lexy remarked, her cheeks warm, looking out of the windows at the leafy square, adorned with a well-kept garden in the centre. 'I imagine it's as imposing inside as everything else your father furnished.'

'I've never been inside it. You'll have to invite us over for me to offer an opinion,' Jace quipped.

'You're welcome to visit any time,' Lexy told him warmly, cheered by the knowledge that they lived only across the square, although she supposed she could hardly confide in Gigi if her marriage was in as much trouble as she believed it was. No, she needed Mel and had already texted her friend to let her know when she would be arriving and where she would be staying.

'Nic didn't sound too enthusiastic about you travelling without him. You're not thinking of ditching him, are you?' Jace asked. 'You make him happy. He only smiles and laughs since you came into his life. I swear he's the most serious Diamandis ever born.'

Lexy's face flamed. 'Of course I'm not,' she declared with as much assurance as she could gather, when in truth she didn't know what she was doing.

And she was no wiser after she and the kids and the nannies piled into the tall town house across the street to be greeted by an honest-to-goodness butler, who introduced himself as Dexter, and a housekeeper called Agnes. Lexy had phoned ahead of their arrival and had been assured that there was a large nursery already prepared for her children and rooms in the staff quarters to house the nanny trio.

The front hall was timeless, from the original Georgian tiles below her feet to the decorative painted panelling on the walls. The furniture was antique, but nothing was gilded or ornate or too large for its place. It was surprisingly plain and fresh, the gracious ambience almost contemporary.

Nic didn't phone her that night and she didn't bother phoning him, having decided that her days of running after Nic Diamandis were over. Perhaps they could separate now but keep it quiet for a few months to keep his family happy, she thought sadly, fighting against her own instincts with all her might. If they broke up, it could be done with dignity and no great drama. After all, love had never been a component of their arrangement. An arrangement, an agreement, were more apt labels than that word 'marriage'. Just because she had chosen to share a bed with Nic and fall back in love with him didn't magically change their arrangement into a real marriage.

It was dinner time two days later before Nic appeared and he hadn't phoned in the interim. She looked up from settling Ezra into his cot because he had been very restless and there Nic stood in the doorway. And her first anxious thought was what had happened to him since she had last seen him? Shadows were etched under his dark eyes, a heavy cloud of stubble darkly outlining his jaw and tense mouth, his tie loose round his unbuttoned shirt collar.

'You look tired,' she said tautly.

'It's been a rough few days since I last saw you,' he conceded heavily, walking over to join her by the cot, clasping Ezra's tiny hand as it immediately reached up to grasp his father's fingers.

A shout sounded from Lily's cot and, moments later, Lily's tousled head appeared above the cot rail. Nic lifted her, gave her a hug and laid her down gently into the cot again while she babbled her nonsense at him, only the occasional syllables sounding as if they could be part of a word. He peered down hopefully into Ethan's cot, but their second son was dead to the world as usual. Nothing woke Ethan up after a busy day.

Lexy studied Nic, wondering what was wrong.

Sheathed in a silvery grey suit that fitted his big powerful physique with the designer precision of Italian tailoring, he took her breath away as he always did. He had a smoulderingly sexy vibe even when he was travel-weary.

He raked long fingers through his cropped black hair. 'I need a shower, a shave—'

'Maybe some sleep?' Lexy suggested.

'No. I have a lot to tell you,' he muttered heavily. 'I'll tell you most of it over dinner.'

Lexy winced. 'Can't you just spill it now?'

'No, I owe you far too much to trot it all out like it's trivial stuff.'

Although she didn't intend to, Lexy found herself following him into the bedroom, a tranquil, beautifully furnished space the very opposite of the gilded grandeur of his father's palatial home on the island. 'Why's this house so different from the one on Faros if it belonged to your father first?' she asked.

He was halfway out of his shirt, his lean brown muscular torso twisting as he swung back to look at her, a wry smile briefly crossing his lips. 'He purchased it just before he died. I renovated it. I hired an interior designer and asked her to respect the house's history. My father didn't appreciate any history but his own.'

Nic scrutinised his wife, a small, slender figure clad in jeans and a tee shirt. She liked plain clothes: he had learned that shopping with her. She had conservative tastes, didn't like anything that screamed high fashion or showed too much of her body. And yet she was beautiful, show-stopping in her own way, with her soft silky golden hair, her delicate curves and glorious aquamarine eyes.

He disappeared into the bathroom and Lexy sank down at the foot of the bed. She relived the depth of pain she had seen in his stunning dark eyes as he'd looked at her and her heart sank. The backs of her eyes burned. Was it simply that he was so unhappy with her that he couldn't hide it? It was ironic that she simply wanted him to be happy, and she had believed he was while they were in Korea and on his family's island. Only, when her happiness depended on having *him* in her life, she was scarcely a disinterested observer. She didn't know how Nic felt when she wasn't around. She didn't think he had missed her because he hadn't phoned since they'd parted in Greece, and she didn't think he was an emotional guy, unless he lost his temper out of impatience and even then he didn't say much, certainly would never be abusive. It was possible that he was emotional deep down inside but that he kept that side of himself buried around her.

Hey, this is the guy who knows that you married him for wealth and security, she reminded herself as she tugged out a dress to change into. She didn't need to fuss over herself when she was never ever going to be competition for Angeliki, but then he didn't seem to find the blonde heiress attractive. She couldn't sit down to eat with him in a stained tee shirt, not unless she was a total lazy slob. Finding the bathroom empty when she emerged, she went for a quick shower to freshen up before she dressed again.

Nic's hair was damp, a fresh shirt hanging open as he pulled on jeans.

'It's funny,' Lexy said ruefully. 'I get dressed up for dinner, you get dressed *down*. It shows what a bad match we are.'

'We're not.' Nic watched her perch at the foot of the bed, her hands linking together in a tight grip that told him she was very tense and anxious. He breathed in deep and strong. 'You know, I missed you—'

'You could've taken me with you,' she reminded him.

'It's just as well that I didn't. I got very, very drunk the night before last and I'm still feeling the effects. I found out a whole lot of distressing things over the past two days and I didn't handle it well.'

Her smooth brow furrowed. 'Distressing?'

'Very distressing and very much a blueprint of my own flaws, so I probably wouldn't have been good at trying to explain it all to you in the frame of mind I was in. I'm not saying that I'll do it any better tonight but at least I'm desperate enough to *try*,' he completed grimly.

'I've been wondering if maybe we should be thinking of...of a er...friendly separation...even if we're living under the same roof,' Lexy proposed shakily. 'I don't want to deprive you of the kids and it's not like I hate you or anything...or you hate me.'

Nic lost all the colour in his bronzed complexion and stared back at her as if she had punched him. 'I don't want a separation—'

'But perhaps it's what we both *need*,' Lexy qualified. 'You're not happy right now and I can see that—'

'Shelve this discussion for now but let me say first that that's not true. I will explain why. Obviously you're unhappy and I don't blame you,' Nic declared flatly. 'But that could change if other things changed—'

'People don't change,' Lexy sighed.

'That depends on their motivation. Let's eat and I'll tell you about Angeliki,' he urged, grasping her hand to tug her up and head her downstairs.

'Angeliki?' she questioned in bewilderment.

'Yes, and my office manager, Leigh, and my mother. I've been talking to all of them in the last couple of days and it was an eye-opening, very unpleasant experience.'

A maid delivered the starter beneath Dexter, the butler's watchful gaze. Lexy lifted her wine glass while Nic pushed his glass away and poured himself some water.

'Angeliki...' Lexy prompted uneasily.

'We grew up together. Her mother, Rhea, is my mother's best friend. It was inevitable that I saw a great deal of Angeliki. She was like a little sister to me. She's a couple of years younger than I am. I...' He hesitated, his lean dark features tightening. 'I loved her as a part of my family. As a teenager, I was quiet, good-living and a disappointment to my father, who would've been delighted if I'd gone wild like Jace did but that was never me. Angeliki was colourful, adventurous and everything I was not, an entertaining companion for the adolescent years.'

'But the friendship remained—'

'Yes, until she tried to get into bed with me a couple of months before I met you and I rejected her. I was shocked by her approach, totally unprepared for that.'

Lexy almost winced because, in some ways, he was still innocent, certainly not always good when it came to reading the room. 'Angeliki has always wanted you for herself. I saw that in her the very first time I met her. So,' she pressed, helpless not to ask. 'Did you sleep with her?'

Nic studied her in wonderment. 'Of course I didn't. It was always platonic on my side of the fence, and she reacted badly to rejection.'

'I can imagine,' Lexy muttered in relief that her own reading of that relationship had been correct.

'For weeks, she wouldn't answer my calls and I felt bad about it. Then my father died and, being Argus, he left a bombshell letter for me, which I received after the will reading. A letter telling me that Angeliki was my half-sister.'

'Good grief!' Lexy gasped, unprepared for that revelation.

'I couldn't face telling her straight after that getting-into-my-bed episode, so I thought I'd let the memory of that fade before I told her the truth.'

Lexy nodded, following that reasoning but shaken too by the sudden awareness that Angeliki, the shrew, was actually a member of Nic's family.

'And then I met *you*,' Nic informed her. 'And that was like casting a stone in a very deep pond because Angeliki got in touch with me again and I told her about meeting you.'

'You told *her* about me?' Lexy repeated in surprise at that admission.

'Yes. Total idiot about women here,' Nic quipped with a curled lip. 'I raved about you like a teenager, according to her, and she realised that I'd finally met what she saw as competition.'

Lexy winced. 'I could never be competition to a woman as gorgeous as Angeliki Bouras.'

'Beauty is in the eye of the beholder, and I saw you as a beauty from the first moment I saw you,' Nic disagreed. 'A beauty with ten times Angeliki's appeal.'

Lexy studied him in astonishment and recognised that he absolutely believed that, believed that she was way more attractive than his half-sister. Of course she was, *now* that he knew Angeliki was family. After all, Nic was laying it on a bit thick because how good could she have looked after that car accident in Yorkshire? Nose and ears red, face white with shock in the cold?

Nic lifted a folder onto the table and pushed it in her direction. 'This is the file that my office manager gave me the day before yesterday. It lists your every phone call and includes your letters...read only by *me*,' he specified with care. 'And that's why I got drunk. After reading those and understanding how alone you felt coping with so much, I was devastated.'

'I don't understand. You're saying that you never received my letters back when I posted them? How can that be? Your office manager? Why would she hold back confidential letters?'

'Angeliki told her that you were a stalker.'

'A...*what*?' Lexy gasped in disbelief.

'She persuaded Leigh that you were a stalker by showing her your photo and told many lies that indicated that you were a woman causing me embarrassment. Leigh only smelt a rat when she saw photos of our wedding.'

'Naïve,' Lexy muttered weakly, thinking of the icily polite lady she had had to speak to when she had been futilely seeking a meeting with Nic at his office. Leigh had never ever been rude or dismissive but had always remained professional and courteous even if she hadn't given an inch.

'No, I think the real problem was that Leigh is kind

of motherly with me.' Nic frowned. 'She's known me since I was a little boy coming into my father's office. When Angeliki told her that a stalker was targeting me, Leigh would have gone into super drive to protect me because she saw that as her job.'

'Right...' Lexy's voice was fading away as the main course was laid in front of her. It looked amazing but her appetite had gone. She sipped her wine instead.

'So, after Leigh had brought me up to date on what had been happening behind my back, I sat down that night and read your unopened letters,' Nic admitted.

Lexy blinked, said nothing, but how *could* she feel when those letters had been written so long ago when she was in a certain frame of mind, a *desperate* frame of mind? In short, she cringed, gulped more wine, sat silent.

'I felt like a four-letter word of a guy reading those letters. I... I was heartbroken. I drank a lot that night. I tried to find solace in something but there was nothing there to comfort me. I let you down. I *failed*. I took the risk and got you pregnant and then I wasn't *there* for you to help, to support,' Nic recounted in a raw undertone. 'Nothing I can do or say can make up for those months you were alone. You did *all* the right things. You tried to get in touch with me, but Angeliki's ploys foiled us both. It didn't occur to me that she had always had access to my phone and had blocked your number. I spent a fortune trying to trace you, trying to find out where you worked, and I failed there as well because I didn't know something as simple as your surname. That says it all.'

'That you weren't thinking any more clearly than I was when we first met,' Lexy chipped in helplessly, thinking back. 'I left you to attend that christening and I lived to regret that.'

'Why?' he asked in surprise. 'You had made a commitment and I respected that.'

'My godchild's parents had a huge fight during the christening party and split up a few weeks after that,' Lexy revealed ruefully. 'And in spite of my texts, I haven't heard from my friend since then, so, yes, with hindsight I was a fool to insist on attending that event.'

'But I respected that…your loyalty to your friend. I accepted it because it was the sort of thing I would have done,' he confessed ruefully.

'Even though it cost us so much?' she almost whispered.

'Yes, because you wouldn't be the woman I fell in love with if you had behaved any differently.'

'Think dinner's over,' Lexy muttered, her entire attention locked to Nic's taut, darkly handsome face, because she was barely able to credit that he could speak so casually about *loving* her. 'How can you just say that?'

Nic tossed his napkin on the table. 'I fell for you the same night I met you.'

As he rose from the table, he signalled Dexter and the older man headed for the exit door. Nic searched her troubled face. 'No pretending now, not any longer,' he breathed. 'You're my ideal woman and I almost lost you. Not once but *twice*.'

Lexy was only emerging from her shock. 'You're saying that you fell for me that night?'

'Yeah, I was as seriously uncool and excited about meeting you as Angeliki accused me of being. I was exactly like a dazzled teenager. Apparently, that's how I was talking about you the day after I met you.'

'Me too,' Lexy admitted as he rounded the table. 'I talked you up to the sky with Mel and then you didn't phone and I cringed at all the stuff I'd said about you.'

Nic gazed down at her, dark eyes glittering and full of longing. 'Do you think I could bring those feelings back?'

Feeling cornered, not quite sure how she should feel after that declaration of love, Lexy frowned, only to be startled when Nic dropped down to his knees beside her. 'I'll do just about anything. I'm so sorry I trusted Angeliki and lost you. It's something that I can never make up for.'

Lexy's hands rose from her lap, unclasped and framed his strong cheekbones, small fingers stretching. 'But perhaps I can consider forgiving you,' she said breathlessly, utterly mesmerised by the dark golden, black-lashed eyes claiming hers.

'Truthfully?' he exclaimed.

'Jury's still out,' she warned him.

'If you will only agree to stay with me as my wife, I promise to be the best husband ever,' he assured her, still on his knees.

'Oh, I'm gonna stay,' Lexy told him with confidence, fingers delving into the luxuriant depths of his black hair. 'I mean, you've got a lot going for you. Honesty, that's a plus…especially when you mess up.'

His dark head bent as he grimaced. 'Yes, I lost the plot. Jace warned me way back that Angeliki was toxic and I didn't listen. That side of her never bothered me because, until recently, it wasn't aimed at me. She won't be a part of our lives in the future.'

'But she's your sister.'

'And far from happy about the fact. After confronting her, I went to see my mother to break the bad news that her best friend had given birth to her husband's child,' he told her tautly. 'And that was anything but fun.'

'I can't imagine,' she murmured, thinking of Bianca's soft, affectionate heart. 'That must've hurt her.'

'Not at all,' Nic disconcerted her by responding. 'She already knew the whole story, had *always* known, which explains why she was constantly careful to remind me that Angeliki was the little sister I had to look after when we were kids. Apparently, it wasn't an affair between Argus and Rhea. He had information about Rhea's husband which would have financially ruined the family…he virtually black-mailed her into bed.'

Lexy winced. 'Oh?'

'He threatened Rhea that he would reveal that bombshell unless she acquiesced,' Nic revealed with strong distaste. 'She gave in and Angeliki was the surprise result. It wrecked Rhea's marriage and there was a divorce.'

Lexy was frowning. 'And your mother actually *knew* that he did that to her best friend?' she exclaimed in bewilderment.

Nic vaulted upright again. 'Yes, we talked and I didn't understand. That's the thing about my mother. She forgave my father no matter what he did. She says he wasn't a good man but that she loved him anyway. He beat her, he beat me and it still didn't change anything.'

'He got physical?' Lexy stood up with a grimace. 'I didn't realise.'

'It's not something you talk about. I learned to stay out of reach when I was quite young. He would fly off the handle if you annoyed him. Mum tried to distract or interrupt him and if that didn't work, she would tell me that my father was in a bad mood and that I had to understand that he was a very busy man.' Nic shrugged in dismissal. 'But that's how I grew up, being bullied and beaten, and I learned fast that if I showed any emotion, he saw that as a weakness.'

Lexy stretched up on tiptoe, her small hand stroking his jawline soothingly. 'I'm sorry. I didn't know.'

'When I met you, I was still living with that conditioning. I knew that I wanted you more than any woman I'd ever met straight away but I couldn't process it. I fell for you that night—it was crazy, but I did. I liked everything about you. You were down to earth and frank and that impressed me. Then...' Nic spread eloquent hands and a wicked grin slashed his lips. 'The sex was incredible and all I wanted was more and more of you and that's what we would have had, had Angeliki not intervened.'

'But she did, and I had the triplets alone but for Mel,' Lexy completed with regret. 'We can't change that but I learned to hate you for that.'

'Could you learn to unlearn it?' Nic prompted very seriously. 'I'm not planning to keep anything from you any more. Perhaps I should've been more honest from the start. Our wedding night wasn't planned... I genuinely was not expecting that to happen.'

'You *made* it happen!' Lexy tossed back at him as he swept her off her feet at the foot of the stairs. 'What happened to the rest of dinner?'

'We gave up on it. I didn't make it happen,' Nic protested as he carried her upstairs like a parcel. 'I guess, I was just overexcited.'

'Yeah, no short memory here...you and all the

supermodels you entertained yourself with while we were apart. I saw you on the Internet with them.'

'But I didn't have sex with a single one of those dates.'

'You expect me to believe that you didn't sleep with any of those gorgeous ladies?' Lexy asked incredulously as he laid her down on the big bed in their bedroom.

'Yes. Since the night I met you, there hasn't been anyone else.'

'But...?'

'At first, I was expecting to find you and I was being faithful,' Nic contended, faint colour edging his high cheekbones. 'And then when I couldn't find you, I was so into *you* that I wasn't attracted to anyone else. I've never slept around. You and I were special and I couldn't move past that. And I was glad I hadn't given way to lust when I finally found you again.'

'Only because I put a solicitor on your trail,' Lexy broke in, but she was thinking about that. About Nic Diamandis with his many options choosing not to have sex with anyone else after her. And she liked that, she liked that so much that she felt light-headed in receipt of that confession. He had been loyal to her even after he had lost hope of seeing her again. He had valued what they had found together. All of a sudden, she could think back to that passionate wedding night and forgive herself for being part of it.

'There wasn't anyone else for me either...although

I can't pretend I had many opportunities to stray,' she whispered. 'Is there a reason why you brought me straight to bed?'

A boyish grin skimmed Nic's mobile mouth. 'The obvious.'

'I like that you're not pretending.'

'I'm done with pretending. I grew up having to pretend that I lived in a perfect family, but the truth is that it was dysfunctional...and violent,' Nic framed tautly. 'And at times, I despised my mother even though I always loved her too. But she took everything my father threw at her and when I talked to her yesterday and she told me that she'd always known about Angeliki being my sister, I felt out of all patience with her.'

'I think I might have been as well,' Lexy said uncertainly. 'But Bianca was very young when she met your father.'

'She told me that she still loved him until the day he died, but she also told me that she stayed with him for *my* benefit,' he admitted with a sardonic twist of his wide sensual mouth. 'She said that if she had tried to divorce him, he would have fought to keep me as his all-important son. He had the power and he would've won, but I didn't like being blamed for her choices.'

'Of course you didn't,' Lexy agreed, linking her fingers with his to tug him down on the bed beside her. 'But maybe you could stop being so judgemental.'

'I need to,' he agreed grimly. 'I wanted you back a month ago. I wanted you on any terms the moment I saw you again.'

'Enough to take me on as a gold-digging wife?'

Nic laughed. 'I wanted you any way I could get you!'

'Me and the kids,' she qualified.

'You're my family,' he said simply. 'My fatal error was wanting you to be perfect and holding all those months we were apart against you. I see in black and white. No shades of grey. I assumed that you were lying to me about having tried to contact me while you were pregnant and I couldn't get past that. I should've given you a clean page and let it go but I wasn't capable of that.'

'Neither was I. I couldn't forgive you either for not coming to my rescue,' Lexy confided gently. 'I thought you were lying too, unable to face up to the situation at the time and unable to admit that either. I still fell back in love with you…'

'Seriously?' Nic prompted in astonishment.

'Oh, totally.' Lexy looked up at him with wry blue-green eyes. 'Don't know what it is about you, but you've got that vibe I can't resist—'

'I love you so much.'

'I'm starting to believe that,' Lexy said, sitting up to begin unbuttoning his shirt. 'You're wearing too many clothes again, Mr Diamandis.'

Never slow to take a hint, Nic straightened, stepping away to remove the shirt and follow with the jeans and the boxers. Lexy wriggled her shoulders and began to try and undo the zip of her dress but Nic got there first, running it down and gently easing the dress up over her head while she kicked off her shoes, peeling down the hold-up stockings she wore.

'Leave those on…they're sexy,' Nic murmured.

Lexy just laughed, watching him come down to her, bronzed and sleek and breathtaking, and her heart stopped inside her for an instant. 'Do you think it's possible to fall in love at first sight?'

'I did.'

He looped her tousled hair back from her brow and leant down to claim her lips with his. 'I fell for you like a ton of bricks. The instant I saw you and you started talking and then you cooked—'

'Major selling point from the guy who can afford a personal chef!' Lexy quipped.

'Everything about you is a major selling point. Your face, your smile, your honesty, loyalty, kindness. Your ability to accept a less than perfect guy.'

'But he's *trying*!'

'I want to deserve you and our children. I need to do a better job than our parents did,' he admitted in a raw undertone.

'And we'll be all the better for it because we know we're not perfect,' she told him soothingly, smoothing a tender hand down over his hard jawline. 'I will never stop loving you, flaws and all.'

'So, you weren't leaving me after all when you came here?'

'Maybe I finally wanted you to sit up and take notice. I was miffed that you didn't want me in Athens with you. But no, I didn't want to leave you. It was more about trying to protect myself from being hurt.'

'I will strive to never hurt you again. I love you. I will always be here for you, from now until the end.' His dark golden eyes were molten with love and tenderness as he claimed her parted lips with his and silence fell as they luxuriated in being together again. Intimacy entwined them heart and body, passion and need zinging through them, joyful pleasure and security entangling them as Nic held her close in the drowsy aftermath. In the middle of the night, they got up to raid the kitchen and recalled that long ago night in Yorkshire.

'No triplets this time,' she warned him when they finally fell back into bed.

'But maybe some day *one* more baby?' he proposed.

'It would take an act of God to persuade me to go through that again,' she warned him ruefully. 'And you can't tell if it will be one baby or more than one.'

'Let's talk about it some other time,' Nic murmured sensibly. 'Did I tell you how much I love you?'

Lexy smiled happily. 'You can tell me again. Over and over and *over* again.'

EPILOGUE

Five years later

LEXY STROLLED OUT onto the bedroom terrace of her brother-in-law's yacht and lifted her binoculars to scrutinise her home on the island of Faros. There had been big changes to the property, which had required a major redesign. It no longer resembled a palace. It was more of a sprawling and comfortable beach house, and it was much better suited to a family with young, active children.

Five children, she reflected in wonderment, marvelling that she was the mother of so many. She had allowed Nic to persuade her to try for another baby and, instead of one baby, they had been blessed with twin girls. So that was that now, they were content that their family was complete. Madison and Ella were non-identical and even as toddlers both had burned with high-octane energy. Madison was blonde like her mother and Ella was dark, but they both had Lexy's aquamarine eye colour. Ezra was very much their babysitter on the beach.

As she squinted through the binoculars, she could see her eldest son standing, hands on hips just like his father, telling the little girls to stop doing something he saw as dangerous. He was very protective of his little sisters. Ethan, meanwhile, a risk-taker to the core, was climbing the steep rocky outcrop at the end of the beach and Lily was sitting far below him with her nose deep in a book, staying well clear of the noise and chaos created by her siblings.

Lexy's mother-in-law, Bianca, was sitting on a rug above the beach, her husband, grey-haired Matteo Rossi, by her side. They were supervising the kids for the weekend while Lexy and Nic took off to Corfu to celebrate Lexy's twenty-seventh birthday with dinner and a night at a club.

A step sounded behind her and her binoculars were tweaked from her grasp.

'You promised that you would relax,' Nic censured, making a nonsense of the stricture when he took the opportunity to lift the binoculars to his own eyes to spy on their family. 'Why did we ever think that a broken leg would put Ethan off climbing?'

'Well, at least we've got a retired doctor on site in case of emergencies,' Lexy quipped, referring to Matteo, the laid-back older man Bianca had married during her sojourn in the country of her birth.

'Yes. I like my stepfather. My mother seems much happier.'

Four years earlier, Bianca had announced that she

was tired of being a Diamandis and needed a change. She had bought an old farmhouse near the village where she had been born in Italy and had pretty much left the trappings of her wealth behind her, with the exception of her frequent flights back to London and Greece to see her grandchildren. Lexy was very fond of her mother-in-law and had interceded with Nic, who had been rather overprotective and suspicious when his mother had first met Matteo.

A childless widower, Matteo was a cheerful man with a terrific sense of humour and a great love for both his second wife and her grandchildren. They took occasional trips back to Italy but had based themselves in Greece since their marriage. Although Bianca still regularly saw her friend, Rhea, Rhea's daughter, Angeliki, carefully avoided the Diamandis tribe for neither of her half-brothers trusted her around their families or friends.

During term-time, Lexy and Nic lived in London, where the children went to school, and summers were always spent on the island, but in between times, they travelled widely. Jace and Gigi and sometimes Matteo and Bianca stepped in to take the children and allow Lexy to go off on occasional business trips with Nic. They had returned to South Korea several times together, exploring and enjoying the freedom of being childfree, however briefly.

Lexy was looking forward to seeing Mel and her husband, Fergus, at the party on Corfu that evening.

They were staying there on their vacation and Lexy would introduce her friends to those of the Diamandis family attending. She couldn't wait to catch up on gossip with Mel.

Lexy stilled as she felt Nic's fingers brush her shoulders and something cold and heavy settled round her throat. 'What on earth?' she gasped, fingers fluttering up to touch the jewel suspended between her breasts. She hurried into the bedroom to look in the mirror and study the large teardrop diamond pendant on a platinum and diamond collar. 'Wow! Snazzy.'

'Happy birthday,' he murmured huskily as he closed both arms round her and eased her slight body back into the solid heat of his. 'I told Jace we'd be late for dinner.'

'Is that so?' Lexy gave a shameless little wriggle of encouragement as she spun in his arms and stretched up to connect her mouth to his.

As he kissed her with hungry intensity, he was also in the act of sliding down the straps on her sun dress and divesting her of it and she laughed, feeling it fall round her bare feet. Her hands slid under his tee shirt to smooth up over his muscular torso. 'I like my gift,' she told him softly. 'It'll go amazingly well with the silver dress I'm wearing tonight.'

'I know. I made Gigi tell me what colour it was.' Nic flung off his tee shirt as Lexy stroked her hands slowly over every part of him within reach, teasing the zip straining at his groin and running it down to release him. 'So forward now, Mrs Diamandis.'

'You have no idea,' she said, pushing him back in the direction of the bed. 'You were in California for a whole week.'

'And you missed me,' Nic gathered with a wicked grin as he hauled off his jeans with enthusiasm.

'I always miss you.'

'I was on the phone so much I didn't think you'd have the chance to miss me,' he teased, hauling her down to him and whisking off her lingerie to seal his mouth to a prominent pink nipple.

'Every time I turned over in bed and you weren't there,' she complained with a faint moan.

And then the conversation died away and the passion took over, their bodies straining together as he drove into her with an urgent groan.

'So I think you're getting something fluffy and four-legged from Gigi…just warning you,' he told her breathlessly as he sprawled back against the tumbled sheets.

Lexy beamed. 'She's been looking for a dog for us for months. The children are at just the right age now to be more responsible and Gigi will have tested him out living with their kids,' she said, her body heavy with relaxation and happiness bubbling through her because Nic was home again and she hated it when he was away.

'Act surprised when she shows you before we get off on Corfu. He's rather big though and lively.'

'Perfect for Ethan.'

'Just like you're perfect for me,' Nic quipped, resting back with a smouldering smile of satisfaction. 'You smoothed away my rough edges.'

'Put you in touch with your inner man,' Lexy slotted in, trying to imitate Jace's deep sardonic drawl while thinking about how much more open Nic had become with his emotions now that he no longer felt that he had to suppress or hide them.

Nic rolled her over and closed both arms round her. 'I love you madly, desperately and for ever, *agapoula mou*.'

'And I love you,' she told him, resting her cheek down on his shoulder. 'Perhaps because you're still impossibly pretty.'

Lexy laughed like a drain as he tickled her in retribution, and they never made dinner at all.

* * * * *

MODERN

Glamour. Power. Passion.

Available Next Month

Carrying A Sicilian Secret Caitlin Crews

His Enemy's Italian Surrender Sharon Kendrick

On His Bride's Terms Abby Green

Engaged In Deception Kim Lawrence

Boss's Heir Demand Jackie Ashenden

Accidental One-Night Baby Julia James

Royal Fiancée Required Kali Anthony

After-Hours Proposal Trish Morey

Amore

Billion-Dollar Invitation Michele Renae

Fling With Her Boss Karin Baine

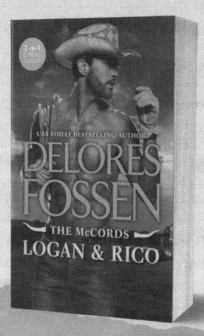

Subscribe and fall in love with a Mills & Boon series today!

You'll be among the first to read stories delivered to your door monthly and enjoy great savings.

MILLS & BOON

JOIN US

Sign up to our newsletter to stay up to date with...

- Exclusive member discount codes
- Competitions
- New release book information
- All the latest news on your favourite authors

Plus...
get $10 off your first order.
What's not to love?

Sign up at **millsandboon.com.au/newsletter**